Bagels and Blackmail

A Small Town Culinary Cozy Mystery

Maple Lane Cozy Mysteries
Book 1

C. A. Phipps

Dedication

This one is for my fabulous readers who stuck by me with this leap into cozy mysteries.

I appreciate this genre is not for those wanting lashings of romance, but I did add a little more this time with you in mind. Hopefully, it will be enough until the next book. 😊

Cheryl x

Bagels and Blackmail

Petnapping in Maple Falls!

Big Red is more than a pet...
... so much more.

It turns out that he's not the only pet taken, which is
a **cat**astrophe for the owners who, like Maddie, consider
them family.

As if that's not enough to cope with, a body is found behind
Maddie's bakery! Naturally, this takes precedence with the
police, but why is no one else searching for the animals?

The Sheriff, who happens to be her ex-boyfriend, is doing
what he can to solve the mystery, but he's too busy and
Maddie can't sit by and wait.

Going against her darling Gran's wishes, she once again

uses her sleuthing talents to piece together the clues—with a little help from her friends.

If you love your pet, this cozy mystery will have you cheering for Maddie, because she won't give in until every animal is home!

The Maple Lane Mysteries are light cozy mysteries featuring a quirky cat-loving bakery owner who discovers she's a talented amateur sleuth.

Other books in The Maple Lane Mysteries
Sugar and Sliced - The Maple Lane Prequel
Book 1 Apple Pie and Arsenic
Book 2 Bagels and Blackmail
Book 3 Cookies and Chaos
Book 4 Doughnuts and Disaster
Book 5 Eclairs and Extortion
Book 6 Fudge and Frenemies
Book 7 Gingerbread and Gunshots
Book 8 Honey Cake and Homicide - preorder now!

Sign up for my new release mailing list and pick up a free recipe book!

> "Enjoyed this book, very engaging and hard to put down. Had to finish it all at once, not easy to stop at any spot besides the ending!"

Chapter One

Madeline Flynn picked up her teacup, inhaling the fragrance that made her warm inside in anticipation of that first sip, while she checked her list, making sure everything was ready for tomorrow.

Moving home to Maple Falls, a small town outside of Portland, Oregon, and opening Maple Lane Bakery with her Gran a few months ago, made her happy beyond words. Fulfillment of her dreams cemented what she'd always known—this was where she truly belonged.

New York City would get along fine without her. Grateful to have learned her trade from the wonderful family run bakery there, credit was still mainly due to her amazing Gran who started Maddie down this road by sharing her exceptional skills. Skills that had augmented the small farm her grandparents owned and ran, selling cakes and cookies to people who came from near and far for them.

Standing on the back doorstep of her magnificent kitchen, she flicked her long, blonde braid over a shoulder as she watched Big Red swat lazily at a butterfly in the afternoon sunshine in their small garden. A Maine coon, she'd found outside her college when he was a tiny kitten and having no idea how big a cat of his breed grew, she'd brought him home. No one claimed him, and Maddie was glad about that every day.

A big eater and even larger than average Maine coon, Maddie adored him. In turn, he offered indifference tempered with affection, depending on his mood. He also ruled the house, something she willingly allowed and to her amusement, so did Gran.

After eleven years, he was her confidant and side-kick, traipsing around town, with or without her, as far as she would let him and further if he thought he could get away with it.

His kitten stage lasted far longer than it should have, and even now he was still constantly breaking things because he had no concept his build did not fit into small spaces the way other cats could. He had also refused to sleep anywhere other than her bed at night, which was nice in the winter, but like sleeping with a thermal blanket in the summer.

He was also a snob. If he liked a person or animal, he could be playful and loving. If not, it was best to keep out of his way. He could fight—he chose not to—but a swipe with a hefty paw, or intentionally walking in front of a person, so they tripped, was his modus operandi, if he was feeling slighted. Or simply annoyed.

And, he was so darn smart, Maddie would swear he understood every word she uttered. That didn't mean he chose to listen or heeded them.

"I'm off home, sweetheart, unless you need me for anything?" Gran came through the curtain that separated the kitchen from the shop, took off her floral apron, and hung it on the hook beside the door. It would be replaced by another as soon as she got inside her cottage which was a gentle walk down the road. Since she didn't drive, the bakery was situated ideally for Gran to come help out most days.

At nearly seventy, she was as spry as someone half her age and could have managed full days like she did when Maddie first opened the shop. Busier than she had dared hope to be, and loving having her around, it wasn't as necessary now that she'd hired her friend Laura.

This meant that Gran, who worked a few hours most days, got to do the other things, besides baking, that she loved. Like getting together with her friends at the community center. She'd tried to pass on the presidency of the committee when the bakery opened so she could help Maddie, but they wouldn't hear of it, and now Gran was back into organizing them as much as she ever did.

"Everything's done. Why don't you take tomorrow off? Laura's doing so well we should be able to manage without you for the whole day occasionally."

Gran sniffed at the perceived slight. "Is that so?"

Maddie drained her cup to hide a smile. "It will be a major struggle, is naturally what I meant."

Laura had come through from the shop and overheard. "I know I won't be anywhere near your ability or speed, Gran, but I'll do the best I can."

Maddie laughed at Laura's earnestness. "Don't pay any attention. She's teasing."

"Oh."

Laura was often very serious because she couldn't always read other people's body language or tone. Fortunately, when she did get the joke, she was able to laugh at herself. This was important because Maddie's circle of friends had made their teasing and quips into an art. It was hard to turn that off even for a relative newcomer in their midst.

Even better than being able to handle the ribbing, Laura turned out to be an incredible find as an all-rounder. Not just as a barista—she was the irrefutable queen of the coffee machine—but also the actual baking side of things, which was arguably the most important.

Together with Gran, they formed a great team. This was despite the initial rocky relationship when Maddie and Laura had been distrustful of each other due to a misunderstanding. That was all water under the bridge, and they were both amazed by the friendship they had discovered.

Laura had been a troubled person when she arrived in Maple Falls to run for Mayor. Having lost the election, she became rudderless, especially when her high achieving family disowned her because she didn't have their drive and ambition in politics.

It was a remarkable twist of fate that brought her to work for Maddie, who was thankful for it and sad in equal measure.

Thankful to have Laura by her side in the bakery so that Gran didn't have to work so hard, and sad because it had come about through the death of a friend who ironically won and became Mayor in that very campaign.

Gran turned at the door. "You'll get used to me, love," she said to Laura. Then to Maddie, "I think I will take the day off tomorrow. I promised Jed Clayton I'd help him look for his Labradoodle. I haven't managed to yet, so now's a good opportunity. I'd hate for him to think I don't care about Sissy."

Laura tucked a stray red curl back into her bun, which was the easiest way to control the unruly curls. "Gosh, is she still missing? The whole yoga class went in search of her the day Mr. Clayton told us in the park. He'll be distraught by now. Those two are as inseparable as Maddie and Big Red."

He might adopt an aloof manner, but there was nothing wrong with her cat's hearing. Thinking he was being offered a treat, he pushed past Maddie and waited in front of Laura who had fallen in love with the massive feline—perhaps because they had similar coloring, or it may be more mercenary—and had taken to heart how he expected to be treated and spoken to, as if he were a person.

Holding out her empty hands, she gave him an apologetic look. "Sorry, I was talking about you, not calling you."

He gave her a withering glance and went back outside, his large fluffy tail flicking with indignation.

Gran snorted as she followed him out. "Pets, even ones with big egos, are better medicine than most pills." Then added on a serious note, "What worries me is how long it's been since Jed's seen Sissy."

"I hate to think anything sinister about it, but I've heard Sissy isn't the only animal that's disappeared lately." Maddie frowned, as she looked at Big Red who'd resumed his butterfly watching. It would be awful to lose your pet, especially when they were a big part of your life and your family.

Gran wagged a finger at her. "Now, don't go looking for trouble. We've had enough intrigue around here to last a lifetime."

"Absolutely, but it makes you wonder if someone is targeting our animals, doesn't it?"

"No, it does not. I'm going home before you start with your suppositions."

Maddie couldn't help but smile at Gran's back. She had no regrets over her involvement when one of their own had been murdered, and she and the Girlz had helped solve the case. Plus, Maddie knew Gran was proud of her but was also protective. She meant nothing by her stern words.

Having seen a lot of life, good and bad, and having dealt with it accordingly, Gran prided herself on focusing on the good. There had been little good about that case, apart from catching the murderer. And Laura joining the Girlz.

The doorbell tinkled out in the shop.

"I'll get it." Maddie went through the curtain where Angeline Broome, aka Angel, was studying the display case. Brightness emanated from her, and it wasn't just about her clothes, which were all about sunshine and rainbows every day. Her blonde, shoulder-length hair shone and bounced around her face. She walked like a model, with legs high-stepping and elegant.

No one could guess at the hard life she had endured. Growing up in a trailer park, then marrying the school jock should have had a happier outcome for the southern bell. Unfortunately, her ex turned out to be a big drinker and became abusive.

Now, Angel was single again, like Maddie, Suzy, and Laura. They were lovingly called the 'Girlz' by Gran and her friends because they were together as much as possible and except for Laura, had laughed and suffered with each other since they were children.

"Good afternoon," Angel almost sang it.

Maddie smiled at her best friend, always happy to see her. "Good afternoon to you. Have you finished for the day?"

"I wish. I've got a couple of the blue brigade coming in very soon. I need a pick-me-up to get me through listening to their mean gossip that falls from them like rain in September. What do you recommend?"

Maddie went to her side of the display case. "Hmmm, no jam doughnuts left. I'm thinking a piece of apple pie might do the trick as a substitute."

"Your award-winning pie is the best substitute I can think of. Can I get one of Laura's cappuccino's too, please?"

While Maddie blushed, which was something she couldn't seem to stop doing when someone praised her work, Laura heard her name and came out of the kitchen.

"To go?" she asked.

Angel was still grinning at Maddie's reaction. "Yes, please."

"I'll have one too, please." Maddie jumped on the order.

Angel raised a perfect eyebrow. "Laura's converted you to coffee? Gran will have a conniption."

Maddie laughed. "Not totally, so no need to stage an intervention just yet. I find it helps around this time of day when it gets a bit slow before closing. How could I possibly stop drinking tea when my shop looks the way it does?"

They studied the old cabinet to the left of the display case. It was full of individual tea sets and teapots, all of which had been lovingly donated by Gran who'd emigrated from England as a child and was an anglophile, through and through. If it was anything to do with the British monarchy, Gran had to have it.

The bakery offered barista coffee thanks to Laura, but before that was even an option they'd served tea and continued to do so in Gran's collection of antique China, and what a collection it was. Although, it didn't include the select pieces she kept at the cottage for friends and family who stopped by.

"True, and it looks stunning. I try to alternate between tea and coffee during the day; otherwise, I can't sleep at night." Maddie picked up her coffee and took a careful sip. "Perfect."

"You really shouldn't have any caffeine after five. I read that somewhere." Laura added apologetically as she handed Maddie her coffee.

"I've heard that too, but I don't like to be told what to do. Ever." Angel winked at them as she left with her coffee and pie.

Maddie sipped the delicious brew and closed her eyes for a second. "You really are an excellent barista."

"Thanks. It's always good to hear. I hope one day you'll be able to say something similar about the way I bake." Laura's cheeks flushed.

The one thing they were so alike in, apart from their love of baking, was this inability to take a compliment. Unfortunately, Laura's issues were more varied than Maddie's and deeply entrenched. Maddie would love to help her friend get over the belief that her opinion couldn't be counted.

"You've learned so much already that I have no doubt I'll be saying it very soon about everything you bake." She glanced up at the clock. "It's nearly time to close, why don't you head home too?"

Laura smiled. "You know I really enjoyed today, even though we've been going non-stop since we opened this morning. Which is fine by me," she added hastily, "because we have so much fun that it hardly feels like work. Isn't it great that sales have picked up over the last few weeks?"

After Maddie's food had been exonerated of being the source of a poisoning, the bakery began to do a roaring trade. This was an incredible relief for Maddie, Gran, and their fledgling business.

"It sure is and I'd like to thank you again for the extra

hours you've been doing. It's removed some of the pressure from Gran since you've taken over the early shifts."

"I'm glad for Gran, but I don't mind at all." Laura hung up her apron and stood awkwardly at the door. "Without sounding indelicate, do you think she'll retire anytime soon?"

"Hah!" Maddie snorted. "Gran has never had an idle day in her life. Still, I'll be happier if we can get her working fewer hours. Even knowing she'll be baking at home anyway."

"That reminds me, did you get any response from the advertisements for staff you put in the local paper?"

Maddie gasped. "Oh my gosh, I can't believe I forgot to tell you. For a change it was an amazing response, and I spoke to all of them last night. The first applicant should be here soon, followed by another two."

"Wow. That's wonderful. Do you want me to stay?"

"No, thanks. I'll close once they arrive. Fingers crossed this bunch will be better than we've had up until now."

Laura clucked her tongue. "I can't believe anyone would ask for a job at a place like this when they don't much like other people, and they aren't interested in learning to bake. Isn't that bizarre?"

Maddie nodded. The last few applicants had seen the bakery more as a place to socialize than work. "More than bizarre, it's a waste of everyone's time."

"Well, good luck, and I'll see you in the morning."

Watching her leave Maddie hoped that she would find another just like Laura. While happy to spend time training someone, she wanted them to have a passion for baking, and also a passion for her customers the way she did.

It was important to have people not only love her food but come into the shop because they enjoy the English oasis she'd tried to create. She'd seen the benefit of creating an atmosphere when she'd done her own internship. Of course, the emphasis in that family bakery had been on French pastries, but it was still relevant no matter the theme.

The doorbell took care of her introspection.

Chapter Two

A young woman hesitated as she entered, nervously looking around the shop, appearing relieved that she was the only person there, apart from Maddie.

She straightened her shoulders and strode up to the counter. One eyebrow was pierced and there was a tattoo just above the elbow of her left arm of an elephant. Her jeans and short-sleeved white blouse were tidy enough, and her streaked red/blonde hair looked clean.

Maddie was already mentally ticking boxes.

"Hi. I'm Beth. I'm here about the job."

Maddie smiled and held her hand out. "I'm Madeline Flynn."

The girl hesitated before taking it. The thin hand quivered, proving her entrance had been laced with bravado.

"Take a seat at the table over there." Maddie picked up a clipboard with a list on it, went to the front door and flicked the sign in the window to closed, then joined Beth at the table.

She hadn't asked a lot of questions when she'd rung to

make a time for the interview, because the shop had been busy, so she had little to go on as to whether Beth was a suitable candidate.

"You said you've worked in retail?"

Beth chewed a chipped nail. "At the mall in Destiny."

"What were you selling?"

"Hair products."

Beth's hair gave the girl some color since she was rather pale and Maddie admired it as she wrote notes. She'd always wanted to be more daring with her own.

"Did you bring your resume?"

Beth shook her head, looking down at her hands on the table, then folded her fingers, presumably to hide the chewed nails.

"I don't have one. I got that job in Destiny through my mom straight from school. I haven't worked anywhere else."

"And why did you leave?"

"They were having a revamp of the store, and apparently I don't fit in looking like this?" She gave a self-deprecating shrug.

It sounded like Beth would take anything, and that wasn't what Maddie was after. "As I said in the advert, I need someone reliable to work the register, but they'll also need to learn how to do basic cooking and over time, cake decorating. Is that something you would be willing to learn?"

"I guess."

Maddie's hopefulness and patience was waning. It was like pulling teeth and if Beth couldn't at least try to look enthusiastic at the interview then what would she be like serving in the shop? She had seen and heard as much as she wanted to.

"I have your details and I'll let you know by the middle of the week about my decision."

"Sure."

Maddie saw Beth to the door and watched her walk down the street, head down. If she was the only suitable candidate then Maddie would be tempted to give her a shot, because she felt sorry for the girl. A teenager, out of school and now out of a job only led to more issues. It happened here in Maple Falls, but in New York City it was a big contributor to crime.

"Good afternoon, Ms. Flynn."

A teenage boy stood on the other side of her also watching Beth walk away.

"I'm so sorry, I was lost in thought and didn't see you. Are you Luke?"

He gave her a lovely smile. "Yes, ma'am."

She liked that respect even if it made her feel a lot older than her twenty-eight years and she immediately warmed to him. Gran liked to say that a smile could get you where you wanted to go and Luke might be proof of that.

"Call me Maddie."

He took her hand and shook firmly—another tick for the boy.

"Please come in and take a seat."

She quickly flipped to a new page while he sat facing into the room, looking about admiringly.

"I've been in here before, and I love all the British decorations."

"Thank you. I'm sorry, there have been so many people through our doors that I can't say I recognize you. Tell me what you think of the food?"

"I love it. I wanted to apply for a job when I first heard

that you were hiring, but . . . Things happened, and I wasn't able to."

She wasn't sure what had stopped him, but she wasn't overly bothered. "Never mind, you're here now. What sort of work have you done?"

He winced. "To be honest, nothing I've done comes close to this. The thing is, I really want a career in baking. I've helped at the harvests for several summers so I'm strong and fit, and I'm happy to start serving, or in any way you need me. I want to learn from the best."

Maddie grinned at the flattery. He was stocky and quite muscular, so perhaps he'd have the stamina needed for early mornings and long days baking, as well as lifting bags of flour. Although, she was none of those things and managed perfectly well. Still, another pair of hands was what she needed. He was eager and pleasant, two qualities that ticked more of the boxes she had her mind set on. Maddie's heart gave a small leap of joy even as she tried to calm herself.

"I think you could fit in around here, Luke, but I have one more person to see before I decide. I'll ring you tomorrow, to let you know either way."

He studied his hands for a moment, seeming to be more worried than disappointed. Then he gave her a pleading look.

"Do you mind if I come in tomorrow to find out? I promise not to cause a scene if you don't choose me."

She bit back a laugh, because she remembered how earnest she had been when applying for her first job. The whole experience was fraught with awkwardness and fear of coming off as a complete idiot.

"That's no problem at all."

Walking him out, Maddie knew that the last applicant

had better be special, because Luke was a real contender. Which left her feeling bad about Beth. As a teenager, Maddie had also searched for her place in the world and needed a helping hand. Not everyone got a scholarship, but everyone deserved a chance to do something that made them happy.

That is, everyone who actually wanted to work.

The third and final applicant proved to be unwilling to learn how to bake and adamant that they expected to do little else except stand behind the register all day. That wouldn't work in a small business such as Maple Lane Bakery. It made the job of choosing that much easier. Luke Chisholm seemed the best fit, although that didn't stop her wishing she could do something for Beth.

It was a shame she couldn't afford to take on two interns.

Chapter Three

All the next day Maddie waited for Luke. By closing time, she was worried when he still hadn't turned up. He'd sounded so eager to take the job and she couldn't help being sorely disappointed that he'd changed his mind.

Packaging up the leftovers she donated to the needy Maddie was checking her list for tomorrow when there was a knock at the kitchen door.

Thinking it was Bernie, the only cab driver in town as well as being employed as the town's landscaper/gardener to keep it looking neat, came around this time of day to pick up the baked goods, she was surprised to find Luke on the doorstep.

With his cheeks flushed, Maddie didn't get the chance to greet him.

"I'm sorry I didn't come earlier," he blurted. "I had some urgent stuff to take care of. I'll never be late again, I promise. That is if you intended to give me the job."

The last part sounded like a plea and because she wanted to believe him, Maddie shrugged off the doubt.

"Well, we didn't state a time for you to come by, did we? That being said, if I give you the job, you'll need to be here every day and on time."

His eyes widened. "I've got it? I mean, yes. I'll definitely be here whenever you need me."

She smiled at his surprise, followed by an endearing eagerness. "In that case, you can have the job. Starting Monday at 7am."

He'd taken a step towards her as if he was going to shake her hand, but something held him back.

"This Monday?" he croaked.

Maddie frowned. "Is that a problem?"

He gave her a small smile. "Not at all. I just wasn't expecting to start so soon."

Warning bells were sounding again. "Do you have another job you need to give notice to?"

"No. It's all good." He backed away to the door. "Really. See you on Monday. And thanks. You won't regret it."

He took off as if someone were chasing him, almost running over Bernie in his haste, who was about to enter.

"Where's the fire?" He joked as he stepped inside.

Maddie shook her head. "Teenagers can make a person feel old and out of the loop, can't they?"

"Quite frankly, they scare the pants off me. And you're so over the hill I can imagine you would feel the same way." He teased. "Was that a friend of yours?"

She laughed. "Starting Monday, he's my latest staff member."

"Good for you. Looks like things are really coming up roses for the bakery."

"As long as they're edible ones, then yes, it is. The box is right here."

Bernie hefted it, one-handed as if it weighed nothing

"Much appreciated. Have a great night." He gave a wave as he headed back to his cab.

Maddie wiped her hands together as if she was brushing flour from them. She wouldn't dwell on the oddity of her new employee's behavior and be thankful that he had accepted the position. She could see he had the desire, and that went a long way in her book.

Besides, she was hungry. Dinner would consist of left-over quiche and salad, but as usual she'd organize Big Red's meal first. He'd been strangely absent this afternoon, and he usually waited at the bottom of the stairs to the two-bedroom upstairs apartment, about this time of day for her to finish work.

She opened a tin of his favorite fish, tapped a spoon on his bowl, then filled it, which should do the trick. Standing in the doorway, she sucked on her pursed lips, making the universal sound calling for cats, dogs, horses, and probably most other animals.

There was no sign of him and Maddie's skin prickled a little. She shook her head at her silliness. He was a cat who liked to think he owned this street and the ones around it. He'd survived New York City and could therefore take care of himself in Maple Falls. No doubt he'd be home when he was good and ready.

By the time she'd eaten, done the dishes and found a recipe for bagels she was thinking of trying, Big Red hadn't returned. Now she really was worried. Her furry friend never missed a meal and was always inside by this time of night, curled up on her lap no matter where she happened to be sitting.

She phoned Gran.

"Is Big Red there by any chance?" she asked, not wanting to project her fears.

Gran called him a few times while Laura went outside the cottage to do the same, but the answer was 'no'.

"That's okay. I'll check outside again. It's a warm night, so he's probably asleep under his favorite hedge."

Having said that for Gran's benefit, Maddie was hopeful when she opened the back door and went down to the hedge at the bottom of the small garden. He wasn't there.

With the long hours she did, Maddie needed sleep, yet she was wide awake with worry. Inside she went upstairs and climbed onto the bed, propping herself up on a couple of pillows, and set her laptop on her knees. Something was eating away at her. Something she didn't want to think about.

Opening the local paper's online newsletter, Maddie got a shock. A body had been found halfway between Maple Falls and the nearest larger town of Destiny down a ravine. Tire tracks indicated that the person's car had swerved and the body had gone through the windscreen.

The reason it held her attention would be the same for any local who read the article. Bodies did not turn up very often, and deaths around here were usually from natural causes. In a town like Maple Falls the population, barely eleven thousand, was predominantly older people. However, it could fluctuate with tourists by half again that number when the seasonal festivals occurred.

Her friend's murder a few months ago had been the first in many years, as far as she knew, and now this. Was it foul play or just a freak accident? Since there appeared to be no other car involved, perhaps it really was the later. She hoped so.

Moving on, she searched for anything related to missing pets.

The result was more shocking than the death. There had been fifteen cases reported in the last three months. The area was wide. From Destiny, south to Maple Falls, and east and west of both.

Mr. Clayton's Sissy was one of the first date wise, and the others were mostly dogs with a couple of exceptions—a western meadowlark and a northern spotted owl taken from the sanctuary near Destiny.

In an article a week ago, a reporter had written a piece stating that all the animals were pedigreed and the birds were on the endangered list.

Feeling bad for the owners, she couldn't help being slightly reassured. Big Red was perhaps less of a pedigree cat than he gave the impression of being, although she didn't know for sure because he'd been a stray. If the person taking them, and that had to be what was happening, only wanted top breeds to sell, then surely it meant there was another reason he was missing.

She bit her lip. Since she couldn't do a thing about conjecture, she continued to read the cold hard facts recorded. Three of the dogs and two of the cats had come home. The owners refused to comment, saying only that they were glad it was all over.

What was over? Had they been prompted to make the same statement by an overzealous reporter? Was it merely something people said when the emotional roller-coaster of losing a pet suddenly stopped? Or was it something more sinister?

Whatever the reason, it didn't tell her anything about how the animals arrived home, and she wondered about the not commenting further angle. Were they scared to say anything? And, if those pets came home, would all the others do the same, given time. Or were these cases unrelated?

After a few hours of this torment, Maddie switched off her laptop and light. It might be Friday night, but she'd been up since 5am and her eyes were gritty with fatigue. She closed them, hoping that Big Red wasn't hurt or cold. Or about to be another statistic.

Mostly, she hoped that he would be home in the morning.

Chapter Four

Throwing on an old cardigan over her nightie, Maddie ran downstairs the moment she got up. She wrenched open the back door and went out into the garden. Pursing her lips she made the calling sound. When that didn't work she called his name softly, then a little louder. Unlike her dream, Big Red hadn't come home in the middle of the night.

With a sigh she went back upstairs to shower and dress. She'd tossed and turned most of the night, which was hardly refreshing. A brisk walk might help.

Unable to stomach breakfast, she headed down Plum Place which ran along the back of the block of four shops, hers at one end. Two doors down was Angel's Salon.

There were three things about Angel that were a given.

1. She was without a doubt, the prettiest woman in town.

2. Angel loved food (which made her the perfect best friend for a baker).

3. Since she also loved her sleep, there was no chance she would be up.

Like Maddie, she lived above her shop. Unlike Maddie, she woke with just enough time for her hair and make-up before starting work and managed to look like she'd stepped out of a magazine. She worked six days most weeks and they were long days, apart from Saturday when she tried to finish at noon.

In this respect they were also a good match, because most Saturday afternoons and Sundays they merely wanted to relax, and rarely went out at night mid-week. It might seem odd for a couple of twenty-eight-year-olds, but right now they were doing what they'd dreamed of and were happy enough with that. It would have been nice if they both had more free time and that might happen even- tually with the addition of the extra staff they both needed.

Maddie stopped at the end of the row, which was the butcher shop, a favorite haunt of Big Red's when he wasn't keeping guard of his own garden at the back of the bakery or visiting Gran.

Half a mile down the end of the street was Gran's cottage where Maddie grew up, after her mom decided that raising a child wasn't the best thing she could do with her life. She had long gotten over the feeling of rejection, because if she was honest it had been a relief not to deal with her mother's up and down personality. Gran was the best parent/grandparent a person could have and Grandad had been just as awesome.

Working for the government in a classified job, he had been capable of turning his hand to anything, and was a shock when he passed.

The cottage was and always had been a haven should she or anyone else ever need it. It had also been Big Red's first home. Now, instead of Maddie and Big Red living with

Gran, Laura did. Which made perfect sense—Laura needed a place to stay and Gran had company.

Being Saturday, the butchers was closed, so she'd been more hopeful than expectant of finding her cat hovering around there.

She carried on, cutting through the library carpark, before heading down Maple Lane along the front of the shops, around by the park and back up Plum Place on the other side of the road, keeping a constant lookout for Big Red.

She walked most days because after her kitchen, being outside in nature was her favorite place to be. As she neared Gran's, the fresh air had helped her anxiety a little. But this was more than a social call.

The door was wide open, the rocking chair empty of Gran or Big Red who usually sat precariously on the back of it whenever he visited. She walked on through the old cottage which had been in the family for three generations.

Gran was in the huge garden with Laura, their heads bent over the same bed of vegetables. Maddie's heart did a little flip, at the red-head so close to the gray, and she allowed herself to acknowledge internally that she was a little envious. This used to be her and Gran out here together, but with everything else, time wouldn't allow for more than tending to her own small garden at the back of the bakery.

Since they lived in the same house, it was natural Gran and Laura would spend more time together, especially with Gran being so caring. In fact, she was the go-to person in Maple Falls for many of the residents and helped so many of them in one way or another.

They were all lucky to have her and it was only right to share the love. Maddie got to spend a lot of time with Gran in the kitchen most days, and Laura deserved family time with people who didn't judge her. Having parents who had dictated her whole life until recently, Laura had been a bundle of neurosis when she came to town and put her hat in the ring for the mayoral race.

With Gran in her life and the rest of Maddie's friends to gently push her, Laura was blossoming into someone more self-assured and capable with every passing day.

Laura looked up and smiled, as if she had heard Maddie's thoughts and approved. The sun glinted off her vibrant red hair and Maddie couldn't help noticing that being happy also made her friend more attractive.

"Did you have a relaxing morning, Maddie?"

She hated to bring them down, and she procrastinated over telling them her fears. "It makes a difference not getting up at five, doesn't it?"

"It sure does. Gran and I had a lazy morning and haven't even had breakfast, but we couldn't resist the sunshine. Can I fix you something?"

"I'm glad both of you managed a bit more rest and I didn't come for breakfast. Ahhh, I have good news and some bad news."

Gran brushed dirt from her gloves and tutted. "We'll have the good first, otherwise the bad is sure to spoil it."

Maddie smiled weakly. "The successful applicant has been offered the job. A young man called Luke Chisholm. Hiring him should make things easier on all of us."

"I wasn't really complaining." Laura's smile was replaced by worry.

Maddie hated that Laura still had these moments of insecurity. "I know, but I feel bad that you two have to work so hard for my dream."

"I'm sure he'll fit in fine, and you do know I'm loving every minute of it? The baking especially."

Gran stood. "Don't talk silly, either of you. We wouldn't do it if we didn't want to. I wish I could have been there for the interview, but the community center committee has been busy with charities, and poor Jed needed some cheering up."

"Sissy is still missing?" Maddie's fingers tapped on her thigh as she felt her fear increasing.

Gran raised an eyebrow at the tapping and tutted when Maddie clasped her hands together to still them.

"Yes, and it's so sad. Now what about this bad news?

Maddie took a big breath. "Did either of you happen to see Big Red this morning?"

Watching Maddie intently, Gran slowly took off her gardening gloves and put them on top of a basket where an array of flowers lay. "Not since yesterday. That cat has a mind of his own, he could be anywhere."

She was trying to put a positive slant on it but Maddie could see she wasn't as convinced as she sounded. Gran was good friends with Mr. Clayton and no doubt they had discussed reasons for Sissy's disappearance.

"I know he likes to wander, but it's not like him to miss dinner, and now breakfast. Perhaps he came and went again before I got up, and he's been fending for himself." She said it as much for herself as for the other two.

"Like eating a bird?" Laura blanched.

Despite their worry, Gran and Maddie snorted. Not only did they look alike, or had done at the same age, but they had the same sense of humor.

"Big Red would never expend the energy to catch anything. I don't think he could get his butt off the ground for a start. Actually, he's just plain lazy. He'd rather go sit on someone's doorstep until they caved in and fed him. He's not fussy either. A piece of meat or a croissant is all the same to him. Although he does draw the line at bagels." Gran wiped the corner of her eye.

"He certainly is a big cat." Laura admitted warily, not always appreciating their jokes.

Maddie smiled. "To be honest, I believe he thinks he's a dog."

"That makes sense. He's certainly big enough to be one." Gran tucked her arm through Maddie's. "All this talk is making me thirsty. Tea anyone?"

Maddie could always drink tea. "Please. I'll give the pound a ring. Just in case."

They went into the kitchen, where Gran's phone hung on the wall as it had for decades.

"I have cupcakes ready to frost, if you're hungry?"

Maddie shook her head as she dialed. "You baked on your day off?"

"I love to bake, no matter the day. You know that."

It was true, and Maddie shouldn't be surprised since she was often guilty of doing exactly that. When you had nothing pressing, it proved to be the perfect time to try out a new recipe or two. They headed into the kitchen which looked out over the garden with the dining room beside it.

"Shall I frost the cupcakes? I could do with the practice." Laura asked.

"Yes, please," Gran answered, as she made the tea in a pot showcasing the royal couple, Prince William and Kate.

The pound had no cat resembling Big Red, so Maddie collected three tea-sets from the shelves, each one a little different. Anyone lucky enough to be invited for tea on a regular basis was designated a particular set which included a side plate. This was a necessity since tea was always accompanied by something from Gran's repertoire of baking which changed with the seasons to coincide with what fruit was available and also with what she felt like making.

Maddie's set had a delicate pink rose depicted on two sides. Gran's had lilacs and now that Laura lived here, she used the blue wisteria pattern.

She sat down at the table, feeling a little edgy that she wasn't out scouring the streets for Big Red, but she was also a little light-headed from lack of sleep and food. The smell of the cupcakes was divine. No wonder Laura was coming along in leaps and bounds in her techniques at the bakery. With Gran as a private mentor, she had already perfected several recipes.

Cupcakes instead of a proper breakfast was not the best as a rule, but on her day off she decided the rules did not apply and therefore had two. "Very nice, Gran, and superb frosting Laura. Is this a new recipe?"

"It is. Coffee and maple syrup. Laura and I have been getting very creative."

"Mmmm. Delicious. The frosting too?"

Laura nodded. "Cupcakes are a good seller at the bakery aren't they?"

"Everyone loves cupcakes," Maddie had to agree.

"You do have a great selection of sweet things," she hesitated.

Maddie could see she had something on her mind. "Any ideas are welcome; we're a team after all."

Laura beamed. "There've been several requests for bagels. Apparently, they're a healthier option and you can add savory or sweet toppings."

"Bagels? What a coincidence."

"No such thing as coincidences," Gran chimed in.

Maddie smiled at the saying. Gran had a million of them.

"I've been trying them out and they're okay, but I need more practice, since I hadn't made them in a while. Bernie's been taking them in the charity box."

"I bet they're better than you think." Gran insisted.

"Maybe. The point is, when I initially chose which items to bake, I didn't include them because I didn't want to have to make too many items with just the two of us working there. I was thinking that since our customers really like their fresh breads and buns, bagels are a natural extension of that. They're another option, and we won't be as stretched for time now we have our new staff member. And another about to start. If you like, we could get some practice in at work and maybe get the cooking class to try the recipe?"

"That would be great. I can't wait. I love bagels. Virginia Bolton was asking about them too, so we know we'll have at least one sale."

Maddie choked on a mouthful of tea at hearing the real estate agent was wanting to eat her food, having denigrated the bakery not so long ago. "I can't say that's an incentive to bake them."

Gran patted Maddie's hand as she passed her a napkin. "Now, now. She's paid her dues. The poor woman has been ostracized by the whole town for long enough, and her business is almost non-existent."

Maddie wiped her face on the napkin, her anger warring with compassion. The fear and drama Virginia helped cause was still too real. "It's only been a few weeks. I can't say that I blame anyone for steering clear of her."

"Maddie, that's not how you were raised."

She dropped her head over the steaming cup at Gran's

censure. Virginia had helped the murderer up to a point and insisted she didn't know how far Ralph Willis was prepared to go to get what he wanted. She had also treated Maddie and her friends badly since they were children.

"Big Red could have been killed."

"But he wasn't. Remember, Virginia has a mother she was protecting. Her reasons were valid to her."

Maddie sighed. "I know, but it's hard to let go of what might have happened if she hadn't come forward when she did."

"There you go. When it was needed, she did the right thing. That's all anyone has to do in this life."

There was no way to fight Gran's brand of optimism or logic, so she changed the subject.

"Regardless of who wants to buy them, how they sell will dictate whether they stay on the schedule or not," she explained to Laura. Finishing her tea, she stood. "I'm going to have another look around for Big Red. If either of you see him, could you give me a call?"

"Of course we will, sweetheart. He'll be back before you know it. Have a lovely day and see you here for dinner tomorrow."

She nodded. "I wouldn't miss it."

Once you gave it some thought, Gran's code of fairness was usually right. Plus, her grandmother lived by that code every single day and, by the number of friends she had, anyone could see the benefit of it.

She left them with a heavy heart, knowing she would be more charitable to Virginia in the future, but more worried about finding Big Red. Sighing, she kept her eyes peeled for any sign of her big ball of fluff.

Calling his name, more times than she cared to count, Maddie walked around the block and down to the small park opposite the side of her corner shop once more, without any luck. It was still too early for most people to be out and about on a Saturday, unless it was festival day, sport, or there was a farmer's market happening.

Maple Falls, with its canopy of large Maple trees creating dappled light everywhere, was quiet and peaceful. The yoga group would be here soon and Maddie wondered for the umpteenth time if she should join them. The one thing stopping her, apart from a smidgeon of laziness, was the idea she might open the shop on Saturdays one day. It was a huge day for sales in the bakery she had previously worked in. In Manhattan, everyone seemed to pour into the shops on the weekend. Still, Maple Falls was perhaps not in that league.

Arriving at her gate, something shining in the grass caught her attention. Instantly she knew what it was. Bending she picked up Big Red's collar and bit her lip. Nobody would be calling her if someone found him because without this they wouldn't know where he belonged, although, most of the town would have heard of Big Red, even if they hadn't met him yet. He was pretty memorable after all.

Then she noticed that the collar was undone-not broken. What did that mean?

Chapter Five

As soon as she was inside, Maddie called Ethan Tanner and explained about Big Red's absence, and her worry that it was somehow linked to the other missing animals. He was a good sheriff, and they had some history, but more importantly he was an old friend.

He was there in fifteen minutes. She'd been on tenterhooks waiting for him to arrive and he barely knocked before she had the door open. His presence alone, made her feel a little better.

"Thanks for coming on your day off."

"A sheriff's always on call," he teased, as he sat on a stool at the huge counter she used for the baking. "I understand you're worried, but there's no reason to think it's foul play just yet."

"Isn't there?" she showed him the collar. "He's a clever cat, but not clever enough to undo this."

Ethan took it and turned it over in his hands. "Perhaps it slipped off and came undone?"

"Not a chance. It was the biggest collar I could find, but

C. A. Phipps

it only just fit him. Plus, it's a buckle, which requires fingers to undo."

He grinned. "Why do you all of a sudden sound like a detective?"

She shrugged. "I've known you long enough to understand that solving a mystery takes a keen eye."

"It's a little early to say that this is more than a missing cat, but I'll alert the station and tell everyone I see. I wouldn't panic just yet. You said you saw him yesterday morning, which is not that long."

"You know he never misses a meal," she said her fingers tapping on the counter.

"True, but I don't think missing a couple will do him any harm." His lips twitched.

"It's not funny, Ethan. Other animals have disappeared too."

His grin slipped. "If you're talking about Jed Clayton's Labradoodle, I wouldn't say that's a good example. Sissy has been known to roam all over town."

"But she's been missing for a month or so, hasn't she? I wouldn't call that 'roaming'."

He sighed. "I agree, it has been a while, but we can't say for sure that she isn't simply lost."

"Which is nearly as bad as being stolen. Here, take a look at this." She slapped the print-outs about the missing animals and the one about the murder. "Do you think these are connected?"

"Wow. I didn't realize there were so many. Funny how the owners haven't been in to lodge complaints. Still, I'm pretty sure lost pets can't be put in the same category as a death or car accident."

"Do you happen to know the name of the person who

36

died? It hasn't been released because they can't contact the family. Maybe they had a missing pet?"

His eyes widened. "That's a pretty tall leap. Please tell me you're not going rogue detective on me again?"

She sniffed. "I could be wrong about them being linked, but I intend to put up posters about Big Red and ask questions around town. There's no harm in being pro-active, is there? And I simply can't wait around like Jed Clayton to see if my boy will come home of his own accord. If you're convinced there's no real foul-play, then it won't hurt anyone, or be dangerous."

He ran his fingers through his hair. He looked different in his jeans and t-shirt. When he wore his uniform it somehow made him all official sounding as well as looking the part. She wasn't sure which look she preferred. Although, whatever he wore and whatever he said, people were inclined to listen to him because he had the kind of presence that commanded it.

Ethan and she had known each other since they were kids and Maddie could see he was struggling between being a friend and being the Sheriff. She appreciated he had a big area to cover, and Big Red's disappearance mightn't be as important, which meant she had no choice but to take matters into her own hands.

Eventually, he nodded. "Okay. Posters and asking around are fine. Anything else is not in your brief, including snooping about that death. Understand?"

"Yes, Sheriff."

He frowned at her easy capitulation. "I mean it. I'll investigate the car accident when I have time, and I'll help you anyway I can, but don't think I won't be watching in case you overstep, Ms. Flynn."

The thought of hunky Ethan watching her every move, made her gulp. "That won't be necessary."

He raised an eyebrow. "Really? Excuse me for finding that hard to believe."

She tossed her braid over her shoulder. "I don't know what you mean."

"You know exactly what I'm talking about."

She raised her eyebrows but thought better about commenting on her inability to let things lay when she'd become involved in helping with Denise's murder, which was clearly his insinuation. This may not be about murder and to some, missing pets might seem trivial, but her heart went out to anyone who lost one.

Ethan knew how determined she could be and was undoubtedly using a Sheriff tactic by waiting for her to capitulate as they stared at each other for a moment. Perhaps he'd feel better if they talked about something else. She knew she would.

"Since we're getting nowhere fast here, I wonder if you might have some information on a teenager called Luke Chisholm?"

His eyes widened at the change of subject or was it something more? He blinked a few times while he thought of a suitable answer.

"What's he done? He's a good kid, or so I hear. I don't know him well, but I've certainly never had any trouble with him."

She shook her head. "As far as I know, he hasn't done anything wrong, which is why I'm asking you. I've offered him the intern job I've been advertising for weeks. He seems nice and he's certainly eager."

Ethan smiled. "That's excellent news. You work too hard. The only reason I'm worried about him at all is because I know his parents. I'm surprised they're okay with him dropping out of college. Throwing away a scholarship and his shot at playing college football wouldn't have gone down well."

"He's in college? I assumed he'd already graduated and had been looking for an opportunity to start a career in baking." Disappointment sucked away her excitement over finding Luke then potentially losing him in a matter of days.

"Hey, don't think the worst. Maybe he lost the scholarship for some reason. Or he got his parents to agree to let him leave. Things have a way of changing in families, so it could be fine."

Maddie frowned. "I hope you're right. I don't want to annoy his parents if working for me hasn't been discussed, but he seemed genuine about wanting to work here. It makes me think about how I'd studied and tried business management before I gave in to my love of baking. I thought how clever Luke is to have chosen his path already. I really want to give him his chance, but I need someone now, not in a few months."

"What did it say on his resume about grades etc.?"

She grimaced. "I forgot to ask him for it."

"You're kidding me?"

"The first applicant didn't have one, and I liked Luke. A lot."

He grinned at her defensiveness. "Yeah, I can see you did and I'm sure that's important. I'm truly not trying to rain on your parade, I just want you to be aware his father has high expectations."

She bristled. "And a bakery might be beneath his son?"

Ethan put both hands up. "Hey, that's not what I think. His father works for Mickey Findlay, and we know what a tough guy he is. Luke's father seems keen to emulate him and have his sons follow suit."

"Oh. Now I am worried. Just because it wasn't proven that Mickey Findlay was involved in Denise's murder doesn't mean he wasn't. I don't want anything to do with the man."

Ethan slid off his stool and came over to where she stood. "You let me worry about Mickey Findlay. If Luke wants the job, then I think it's great you're giving him the break he needs. Just be sure he's doing it for the right reasons and make sure you're not ruffling feathers is all I'm saying."

She screwed up her face. "The last time you said that things turned to custard around here."

He grinned. "I'm sure that had nothing to do with me. I'll leave you to your posters while I get the information about Big Red to the station."

She followed him to the door. "Thanks Ethan. This is important to me."

"I know. That's why I'm doing it," he said with a gentler smile.

Chapter Six

Maddie stood on the back steps, staring after Ethan as he drove off. He was so kind and thoughtful. She was glad their differences from the past had been resolved. Maybe they hadn't worked as a couple, all those years ago, but they'd managed to rekindle their friendship which had turned out to be more important to her than she had realized.

A flash of color in the other direction caught her eye. Angel, wearing clothes even brighter than usual—you could probably see her coming from one end of the town to the other—her hair and make-up perfect, was coming up her walk.

"I saw Ethan's car and got worried, so I thought I'd better check that you're okay, unless it was a social visit?"

She waggled her eyebrows and Maddie shook her head at her friend's unsubtle way of matchmaking, feeling her cheeks redden because of it, but certainly no other reason. She might be annoyed if Angel wasn't so comical about things like this.

"Stop that. Big Red is missing. Naturally I'd call Ethan."

"Oh my." Angel threw her arms around Maddie. "Since when?"

"I'm not entirely sure, but I haven't seen him since yesterday morning," she said with a shaky voice. Angel's well-meant sympathy could often have this kind of consequence.

Angel gasped. "He missed a meal?"

"Two. Thank goodness someone else gets how relevant that is."

"Well, sure. He's a big boy and he needs to keep his strength up. I wonder where he is." She looked around her with particular attention to his favorite place in the bottom of the hedge.

"The thing is, with all these animals missing, I'm frightened that he's been taken."

Angel was shocked once more. "There are others missing? Other than Sissy and Big Red?"

Maddie led her inside and handed her the papers she'd shown Ethan.

"This is terrible."

"There's something else. I found his collar which was undone. I don't know why I didn't notice it in the grass sooner. Maybe I wasn't looking as hard because I really hoped he'd be at Grans, or somewhere in the vicinity."

"Don't think the worst. Maybe he caught it on something and wriggled enough to loosen it. Then he went for a walk and lost track of the time. You know how it is. You get chatting and before you know it you're late." She tried a grin.

Maddie shook her head. "Ahhh, he doesn't actually speak so people can understand him."

"Except for us," her friend added seriously.

Angel was a happy pill you didn't need a prescription

for and Maddie had to smile about that. She wouldn't make a habit of telling anyone else about the perception of understanding a cats' language, but Angel was not just anyone and Big Red loved her too.

"He does have a way of letting you know exactly what he thinks."

"Since you've moved back from New York City he's been even more vocal. I've watched him terrorize the local cats and even the dogs are wary of him. He seems to have lost any patience he once had."

Maddie snorted. "You can say that again. I guess he prefers his own company too much. Some of the delivery men haven't been impressed. They've taken to bringing things in by the shop door."

Despite their worry they were laughing hard.

"Grown men afraid of a bitty cat!" Maddie wiped a tear from the corner of her eye.

Angel held her sides as she squealed. "More like a small lion. I need to sit down. I don't suppose there's anything to eat around here?"

"Nope. Nothing to eat in a bakery."

"Dry crackers and water?"

"If you want, but I just remembered I do have some left-over carrot cake in the walk-in chiller. Only if you don't mind?"

Angel was already up out of her chair and headed to the silver kettle purchased and sent via Gran's brother all the way from England.

"I guess if there's no doughnuts then carrot cake will have to do, and we better have tea."

"Of course. You get the cups while I get the cake."

While Angel made tea, Maddie went into the walk in and brought out the cake. There was no way she could eat anything else just now, but she cut a generous slice and put it on the matching side plate. One of the wonderful things about having Angel for a best friend, and there were many, was her love of food. Anything Maddie made was eaten with such relish, there was no way a person could ever believe it wasn't first class and therefore gave this baker a wonderful boost to her ego every time.

When she was done Angel set her fork to the side of her plate in a ladylike way as if she hadn't just devoured her portion in record time and smacked her lips.

"I swear your baking gets better every time I eat it."

Maddie grinned. She'd heard this a million times. "Let's hope that's an ever-increasing upward trend."

Angel wiped her mouth and hands delicately on a napkin. "I can't wait for our next cooking lesson tonight."

Maddie was holding a class for her close friends. It was informal and free, but she could see the potential of doing more once she had Luke up to speed, and if there was enough interest. If it worked out that she had the time, then she would charge a fee and make it a side business. So far, the one she was running was fun, but it had only been a few weeks, and she was nervous about committing further energy into another venture just yet.

Angel sipped her tea. "In the meantime, what are we going to do about finding Big Red?"

"We?" Maddie queried and received a disbelieving look.

"Yes, we. If we can solve a murder, we can certainly find a cat."

Maddie pursed her lips. "Ethan said it was too early to worry."

"That's because he doesn't have a pet or a child. He has no way of knowing how you feel."

It made sense and she really didn't need much encouragement. "Four hands are better than two. I'm going to make up some flyers and get them out around town first thing tomorrow."

"Great. I'll put one up in my shop and walk around Maple Lane dropping them off at the houses and businesses. Most of those won't be open until Monday, but we might see other people on our travels."

Maddie felt a surge of excitement. "I'd already decided to go door to door locally. He might have been nosey and accidentally got himself locked in a shed or a garage. If people don't need to go in them, they probably won't think to look unless someone asks."

"Great idea. Let's get the other two involved. With her connections at the school, and various committees she's on, Suzy will be a big help."

They both grinned. Suzy was the local school principal, which highly amused Angel and Maddie. Being at school together, the three of them had never been fond of their principal.

Retired, and running for mayor, Maude Oliver, was currently the President of the Maple Falls Country Club and still capable of making them shake in their shoes. Suzy was a pleasant contrast. Diplomatic and fair, she could be firm when needed. More importantly, she was a huge hit with children and parents alike.

"I'm sure Laura will be happy to help in other ways too. She adores Big Red. Do you need a hand making the flyers?" Angel asked.

"I'd appreciate it. You don't think I'm overreacting?"

"Not at all. Your idea that he's managed to get stuck under a house or in a shed somewhere and can't get out is highly plausible. Either way it will alert people to check and if he turns up by himself, then that's an even better scenario."

Maddie and Angel clinked their teacups, drank deep, and moved into the small alcove where the computer and printer lived.

Between them they worded it as positively as they could and before long they had a recent picture of Big Red on fifty flyers. It could be noted that she had several (hundred) pictures to choose from, but Angel didn't bat an eyelid at that.

'Have you seen Big Red? He is definitely a cat, and yes he's huge. He shouldn't be too hard to spot and since he's a curious fellow he may have wandered into your shed or garage. Sorry! If you find him, please phone Madeline Flynn at Maple Lane Bakery. Thank you.'

She also added her phone number and e-mail address at the bottom in case a stranger to town found him.

"It looks great." Angel picked up a couple of pieces of spare paper and two pens, handing one of each to Maddie. "Let's get a list together of people to ring."

Maddie, self-confessed queen of lists, appreciated her enthusiasm. After running out of names of people they were friendly with, Angel took half of the pile of flyers and names and put them together. She was about to leave when Maddie remembered she had something to discuss with her.

"Before you go, I was wondering if you're still looking for help in the salon?"

Her friend stopped at the door. "Definitely. Did you have someone in mind?"

"I do. How do you feel about piercings and tattoos?"

Angel tilted her head, then grinned. "They don't do much for me, but growing up like I did in a trailer park, it's a lot easier to look past them. I'd be more interested in how they relate to customers and what their personal hygiene is like. You can't have a client tucked under your armpit while you're shampooing if it's not as it should be."

Maddie grinned. "I couldn't agree more. I've chosen the person I'm going to hire from the three who applied. Luke was the better fit for me. The girl I think would suit you seemed eager to try anything. She wouldn't have any experience in hair salons. Is that an issue?"

"Naturally, experience would be preferable, but with so few people needing work in Maple Falls at the moment, I'm willing to give her a trial. Having someone to answer the phone, clean up, and do the shampooing, would make me happy for now. If you think she'll be okay, can you go ahead and set up a meeting?"

Maddie found the number she had for Beth and handed it to Angel. "Remember, I only met her once, so I can't make promises she'll be any good."

"Sometimes people just need a chance and goodness knows I felt that would never happen when I was young."

She gave Maddie a wink and a wave. It was nice to think Angel and Beth could benefit from being brought together, which in turn made Maddie feel more positive about everything else.

Hope and positive friends were a great combination. Like fresh berries and cream.

Chapter Seven

Wiping down the food preparation counter, Maddie placed a vase of flowers she'd picked earlier from her small garden behind the shop. Even wildflowers, which at any other time would have given her a boost, couldn't lift her spirits. Being out in the garden made her even more aware of Big Red's absence. He'd taken to watching her from under his hedge, making sure she wasn't leaving without him, or more importantly, watching to see if she was bringing him food.

She'd thought about cancelling tonight's baking class, but it had become, in the few weeks since its inception, such a regular and important feature of their lives that she couldn't do it.

Madeline Flynn did not usually feel sorry for herself. Living the dream of owning her own bakery, having a group of friends she loved like family, and a grandmother second to none, should be more than enough. She knew it would be again—when she had Big Red by her side.

A day without him was hard. More was proving unbearable.

He was her best friend, apart from Angel and Suzy, and had proved to be in so many ways when she had moved to New York City. It had been a giant leap from small town Maple Falls.

Knowing no one initially, he had endured her rants over the job she didn't like and the rudeness of cabbies. He walked with her through the park and to the shops, waiting patiently for her to emerge with some tidbit for both of them. He snuggled with her during storms and reluctantly played with string she dangled just to humor her, because it really was beneath him.

The few days it had been were far too long. Was it too long for the outcome to be good? No, she wouldn't allow herself to go down that rabbit hole.

A knock at the kitchen door heralded the first member of the group. She didn't bother to let them in, because the door was open as usual, the knock a mere formality.

Angel entered in a bounce of chatter, wrapping herself around Maddie, and squeezed.

"How are you doing, Sugar? I brought your favorite nougat and some peppermint tea to give you a boost. Shall I make a cup now? You look tired. Sit down and I'll bring you some."

Maddie did not want tea, which was a rarity. She didn't want any fuss and definitely didn't want to be rude. "Not right now, thanks." She extricated herself and went to the massive pantry to get the last of the supplies they needed and rid herself of this rising irritation of not doing enough.

Angel had always gone overboard in her concern for everything and everyone, especially Maddie. That's simply the way she was, and Maddie wouldn't change her for the world.

With no sign of Big Red and the resulting lack of sleep,

she was grateful to have these three women as her friends and would hate to ruin their night by being a Debbie downer.

She came back with a smile on her face. "What do you think of the recipe I chose for tonight?"

Angel sighed. "I would rather have made the scones you talked about last week. Bagels look harder, so I hope I don't muck it up."

"Think positive, the way you do about everything else. Did you read it through?"

"I did. It looks very healthy."

"That's the idea. I want to sell them in the shop, so you lot are my guinea pigs."

"Charming. I hope you don't intend to sell the ones I make?"

"I wouldn't dream of it."

Angel wrinkled her nose. "Hmm. I'm not sure how to take that."

Suzy, and Laura arrived just then and interrupted their banter. The usual cacophony of greetings ensued. Eventually, they settled down into their places while Angel poured them wine.

Maddie stood and smiled at these wonderful women. "Ready to bake?"

Their faces lit up, and they picked up their recipes from the well-equipped counter she'd previously set up with everything they would need.

"As you can see, tonight's bake is one you weren't expecting, but I'm sure you'll do just fine. Bagels are a healthier carb option and as I told Angel, something I'd like to sell in the bakery. As usual, you'll be making your own to take home. Although, since you can make them with different flavors and toppings, you might like to try each other's."

Suzy grinned. "My grandfather will be so happy if I bring him something I made that's edible. Since grandma passed away, he's always complaining about the food I bring him."

Her grandfather was living in the retirement community and good friends with Jed Clayton. Mr. Barnes senior was extremely jealous of Mr. Clayton's close friendship with Gran and the baking which came his way, so Suzy stopped by the bakery regularly to get him treats.

"I'd be happy if I made one thing that looked like it was supposed to. Although, taste would also be a factor."

They all laughed, except Laura who seemed to be lost in thought.

A space had been set out for each, including one for herself, with the utensils and ingredients they would use in the middle of the counter.

"Aprons on? Check the oven is at the correct temperature. Okay, here we go. Yeast, sugar, and warm water in a bowl."

She added her measured ingredients, mixing them together while the Girlz watched carefully and copied each step.

"Now we'll leave it to stand for three minutes. While that's doing what it needs to, let's get all the other ingredients ready."

"It takes a long time to cook, doesn't it?" Angel pointed at the time of 2 hours written on the recipe.

"It is a little longer than usual, but to make them right, that's how long it takes. Those making cinnamon raisin bagels can add those ingredients after we've mixed in the yeast to the flour."

The level of concentration was amusing, but Maddie wouldn't laugh. There are lots of firsts in life and in her opinion, with the right encouragement, people were happy to try a thing more than once even if it didn't quite go to plan that first time.

"Now comes the good part. We're going to knead the mixture for five minutes." She waited for the groans to subside. "It may seem hard at first, but it gets easier after a bit, and the bonus is, it's good for bingo wings."

Laura grinned as she gave her dough a workout. She truly came alive once they began to bake, and was rightly proud of her newfound talents, although she tried hard not to show it.

Suzy took a moment to check the flabbiness of her upper arms before giving the mixture wary attention, while Angel, tongue clamped between her teeth, began to poke her dough. It could have had something to do with the plastic gloves she insisted on wearing to protect her manicured nails which made her look so awkward. Or perhaps it was the way her bowl slid around her space with the sporadic force being exerted on it.

Maddie stopped her for a moment and put a kitchen cloth underneath the wayward bowl. "That'll help keep it in one place."

Angel looked around at the others who didn't seem to need a cloth, shrugged, then went back to her interpretation of kneading the dough.

Once they were done, it was time to let the mixture rest.

"More wine?" Suzy suggested, already on her way to the walk-in chiller.

It was the only day of the week that any of them drank, as far as Maddie knew, and they rarely had more than two glasses each.

"Any more thoughts on running a paid class?" Suzy asked as she returned. "Plenty would like to join."

"Really? I have been thinking about that, but I'm not ready to commit to it yet. I'll wait and see how my new employee does first and searching for Big Red is keeping me busy enough right now."

Angel noted the slight wobble to her voice and changed the subject to hiring new staff.

"Maddie has given me the number for a young woman, and I rang her. She's coming in Monday for an interview. She sounded very excited and that makes me excited. Imagine if Beth and Luke, Maddie's intern, turn out to be as good as we hope, how much easier things will be."

Laura and Suzy were excited too—for different reason. Suzy, because she was happy if they were happy and Laura, because as she'd explained, she didn't want Gran to work so hard. Both made Maddie's heart swell.

When the mixture had doubled in size, Maddie grinned. "Now for the fun part. We are going to punch this mixture until it says 'uncle'. If you have something niggling away at you, this is the time to let it all out."

Suzy winked. "Oh, I'm going to like this part."

"Me too," Laura added.

Naturally, they had to wait for Angel, who apparently, couldn't bring herself to hurt her mixture. Maddie sighed at the tentative punching going on beside her.

"You can't break anything."

Angel moved her tongue from between her teeth for the length of time it took to comment, "I want them to be perfect."

"Of course you do, but we aren't planning on finishing tomorrow. Are we?"

Angel did not look convinced as Maddie told them to

divide their mixtures into twelve balls, still opting for a delicate approach.

Patience is a virtue', Maddie kept repeating in her head.

With four pots already boiling on the top of the range, they made bagel circles and carefully dropped them into the water a couple at a time. A few squeals, and oohs and ahhs later, it was time to add the toppings.

Maddie's industrial range was her pride and joy. It had plenty of room in the twin double capacity ovens for everyone's trays and nothing could match the look of happiness on their faces as the Girlz put their bagels inside.

As they washed up, Suzy shook her head. "I feel like that was a great achievement and I haven't tasted them yet. It's kind of weird at my age not being able to bake."

Maddie shrugged. "It's not weird. That's the world we live in. Most women have been working full-time over a couple of generations. The recipes and the time spent showing us how, went by the way-side in favor of ease, which includes packaged or prepared foods."

"Not forgetting takeaways, my personal favorite," Angel added.

"I guess that's true, but you learned," Suzy pointed out to Maddie.

"I was an only child, living with a wonderful cook. Gran spent an awful lot of time showing me how to bake so I could help her with her orders. Occasionally I'd want to do other things, but mainly I loved every minute of it." She grimaced. "Apart from the washing up."

Angel nodded. "No one likes that. My mom was a terrible cook, so we had lots of packaged food. Therefore, very few dishes. It was years before I had fresh vegetables, and I never knew there were so many because I'd never heard of them."

Suzy and Maddie knew the story, but Laura was shocked.

"It's true," said Maddie. "I can remember when our friend survived on noodles, and Gran's baking when she could get it."

"Which, believe me, was half the reason I hung around you so much," Angel teased.

Maddie poked her tongue out, while Laura was still trying to come to terms with what she'd heard.

"How did you get such a great figure eating that kind of food?"

Angel shrugged, having been asked this question many times. "Genetics. One of the few good things that came from my parents. Let's not go there, okay?" she grinned, taking the sting from her words.

Laura nodded. "I guess you can't compare environments. We had a cook, so I never had to worry about what food to eat or how it was cooked. Although, I was reminded often enough I shouldn't eat too much because I'd get fat and no one would like me. The past always leaves a mark, doesn't it?"

Maddie could empathize since she'd been left with Gran when she was only ten, and Ava Flynn had never really been a mother in any way that mattered. Preferring to drink and party, small town Maple Falls had lost its appeal for her, if it had ever had any.

She sighed, "It can if we let it. We don't get to choose our family, which is good and bad sometimes. After all, I couldn't have asked for better than Gran. She's my hero. She loves all of you too and considers the Girlz her family."

Pink cheeked, Angel's eyes glistened. "Thanks, Maddie. With parents like mine, it was a relief to be anywhere other than home. Your cottage was and still is my haven. I'm so glad we moved here when we did and you were happy to be my friend. Being called trailer trash all those years often sucked the joy out of everything, which didn't change until I had you and Suzy in my life. And now Laura."

Maddie clucked her tongue, the way Gran did. "And that would have been a crying shame, because you're the most upbeat person I know, who makes us all feel better about most things."

"Aww shucks. I love you too. All of you."

Angel was sniffling into a tissue, and the others looked like they were headed that way too. Maddie wasn't sure how it had descended into a pity party. This wouldn't do at all.

"All right, enough of this bonding. Let's talk about what to bake next week."

"Chocolate cake." Angel dabbed at her eyes.

Suzy shook her head in exasperation. "You say that every week."

"What can I tell you? I love chocolate cake."

"A little bit more practice is needed before we tackle that," Maddie insisted.

"How about chocolate layer cake?"

Maddie snorted. "No."

"We could make scones." Laura took a healthy swig of her wine. "They're easy, and we had planned on making them."

Maddie nodded. "Good call. Scones it is. Some can make savory and some sweet and you can share the results like today. How does that sound?"

Angel patted her stomach. "Delicious. Although, I'll apologize now to whoever shares mine."

Maddie flicked her with a tea-towel just as the timer sounded. Beating the rush to the oven, she made them stand back while she opened the door. The smell had been wonderful while the bagels cooked, now it was heaven as the warm smell of baked bread wafted around them. They were golden brown and shiny.

"Look at your beauties," she said as she pulled hers out first then handed the oven mitts to Laura. "Everyone can get out their own and place them on the trivets in front of your station, so you know which yours is. Be careful not to burn yourselves." She moved back, waiting until they'd done so. "Let's sit down and finish our drinks while we wait for them to cool."

After a while Maddie tested hers and found it cool enough to taste and encouraged them to do the same.

"Oh, my goodness. I made something pretty darn good." Angel exclaimed, as she scoffed a whole one, uncaring about the crumbs which she dabbed at with a finger and slipped into her mouth.

Maddie laughed. "You all did, and you should be proud of yourselves. You can put your bagels into your containers, and we are done. Just remember bagels are just as good with a cup of tea."

This brought a bunch of groans, since they all preferred coffee except Maddie. Over time with her shop looking so English in decor thanks to Gran, and the variety of tea on offer, they had succumbed and now drank it regularly. Still, they liked to tease her about her lineage, especially Suzy and Angel. As children they had thought Gran was fascinating with her slight English accent and were bemused by some of the sayings which naturally Maddie had adopted.

"Thanks so much for tonight. It's been the highlight of my week," she said sincerely.

"I'm sure we got way more out of it than you did. I'll be

by tomorrow to see how you are, and then shall we drop off the flyers?"

"That would be awesome, Angel."

"I'll come too," Laura added.

Suzy frowned. "I wish I could, but there's an emergency meeting about the mayor's position. It's been dragging on and we must get it sorted right away."

Maddie hugged her. "Good luck with that. I can't say I envy you."

"I know where I'd rather be," her friend laughed.

She watched them leave, appreciating how darn lucky she was to have her Girlz. They'd managed to take her mind off Big Red for some of the evening, and she knew they would be doing what they could to spread the word tomorrow and every day until he was found.

Chapter Eight

First thing Sunday morning, Angel arrived bright eyed and stunning in leggings and a baggy sweater that would have looked frumpy on anyone else. As she walked, her hair bounced softly on the fuchsia pink cashmere scarf around her neck. She also wore a small backpack.

Laura wasn't far behind in her designer jeans and navy trench coat. Her red hair was in its usual bun, but the sun shone on it making it sparkle and with the smattering of freckles across her nose, she looked a lot younger than thirty.

"It's a bit cool out this morning, but the sun is shining." Angel looked around the kitchen as she spoke, her voice hopeful, even though she didn't ask the dreaded question.

"He's not back. Do you mind if we leave right away?"

"Whenever you're ready, Sugar."

Maddie wore faded jeans and a jumper Gran had knitted which sported a picture of Big Red on the front. Tucking a blue scarf around her neck, she put on the hat to match her jumper, picked up her shoulder bag which contained everything she could think of, including water, and they headed down Plum Place towards the park.

Ethan and his nephews were there, throwing a frisbee in a very rough and boisterous way. Judging by the squeals and Ethan's laughter they were having a great deal of fun.

Ethan saw them and jogged over. "Ladies," he nodded at Laura and Angel, then turned to Maddie. "I was planning to stop by as soon as I wore these two out a little. Any news?"

She shook her head and pulled the ends of her scarf. "We're off to put up posters and drop flyers."

"Want some more help?" His blue eyes twinkled as he gave her his dimpled smile.

"Only if you have the time," she smiled back.

"I'll just check with the brats, but I'm pretty sure, they'll find it more exciting, than being stuck with me while their mom works."

He ran across the road, looking very handsome and sporty in his black joggers and navy sweater.

The boys were tumbling on the grass still damp with dew, fighting over the frisbee. Ethan picked them up by the back of their jackets and pulled them to their feet. He collected the frisbee and knelt in front of them.

The three women laughed quietly, as the boys scuffed the grass at the telling off they were no doubt receiving.

Laura sighed. "He's a wonderful uncle, no matter what he says about them."

"He is. They listen to him, which is a good thing, and they're good boys really," Angel agreed. "I wonder how he tells them apart?"

"James has a small scar over his right eyebrow. "Laura gave a small laugh. "I believe his brother helped that along."

Maddie wanted to ask her how she knew this, but the boys looked over at the women and nodding their heads enthusiastically at whatever Ethan was saying, the three of them crossed the road.

"Hello boys. Thanks for helping me out."

"Uncle Ethan said we can be honorable detectives this morning," James said, with importance.

Ethan's mouth twitched. "I believe I said 'honorary', but I guess that's close enough."

Maddie bit back a laugh. "We have flyers and posters which we need to give to people, put in letter boxes, or staple onto lampposts."

"Staple!" they shouted; hands out ready for the deadly weapon.

Ethan smacked his forehead. "What have I done?"

"Laura and I can take them with us down Maple Lane, to do the posters, if you two want to drop the flyers?"

Maddie felt her cheeks flame at Angel's unsubtle matchmaking, while Ethan looked particularly pleased and spoke up before she could think of a reason why they shouldn't be alone together.

"Perfect. They'll behave for you, and Maddie and I will cover more ground on our own."

As much as she didn't like being organized, Maddie could find no fault with his logic, and her heart beat a little faster as they headed down the street.

Noah Jackson jogged towards them and when he stopped to chat, Maddie took the opportunity to hand him a flyer.

He frowned. "This is terrible. Maybe you'd like to come on the show and put the word over the air? People need to know they should be careful, and to be aware of any strangers hanging around. I could fit you in on Tuesday?"

Noah was not only the yoga instructor, he was also the town DJ and ran a small station. He often had guests, and even though the idea of it made her break into a sweat, she knew it could have more of a far-reaching impact than her flyers.

"Thanks, Noah. Let me know the time and I'll be there."

"If you bring more flyers, I'll hand them out, scan one, and put it on my website."

"That would be awesome."

"No problem," he called as he jogged up Maple Lane.

Walking around the outskirts of the main streets until all the flyers and her water were gone, they discussed the pet situation in depth. Ethan seemed convinced the murder wasn't connected to the kidnapping, but Maddie wasn't so sure.

"Do you think the pets still missing will be found?"

Ethan stopped, reached out, and tucked a strand of hair back under her hat. "I sure hope so. We'd better head back, so I can collect Jessie and James, and see if Angel is still smiling."

Maddie's cheeks had become warm at his touch, but she grinned. "How could you ever doubt that?"

"Let me see . . . Ten-year-old boys who find it impossible to be still for more than a few seconds at a time, or not to touch something they shouldn't, can damage the psyche of anyone."

"My money's on Angel."

He raised an eyebrow. "I'll take that bet and raise you a dinner."

"A dinner?" The thought of going out with Ethan due to Angel's potential issues with the boys seemed a little odd.

He gave a wry grin. "Okay, it might not have been the cleanest of segue's, so just to be sure—I'm asking you on a date."

They began to walk again, and she appreciated he gave her time to digest it, but she owed him an answer. Her fingers tapped against her thigh.

"I won't pretend I don't think about it, but I wonder if we're really ready to date?"

"I think we are, and I haven't made a secret that I've been ready for a while. What's holding you back?" he said, without rancor.

"Our history?"

"Still? That's just what it is. History."

"I don't want to lose this friendship."

"I might have been angry with you when you left town, but I never stopped caring. Isn't there room for more in your life than the bakery?"

"I care about you too, Ethan, but the bakery is important. Very important. Then there's Gran and the Girlz. But right now, I can't think past getting Big Red back."

"I understand."

"I'm not sure you can. He means so much to me I can barely sleep or eat. Nearly every moment I think of him, and it hurts."

He was quiet for a moment, then said so softly she almost missed it. "That's how I felt when you left Maple Falls."

Maddie was stunned by his admission and stopped mid-stride to face him. "You never said."

His dimple flashed. "It would have been difficult since we weren't speaking."

She waved away his attempt at flippancy. "I'm so sorry.

I didn't understand. If anything, I thought you couldn't bear to see me again."

He nodded. "I guess that was kind of true. I couldn't stop you leaving, and seeing you was bitter-sweet. A reminder of what couldn't be."

The almost poetic prose had her reeling. He'd been a stubborn teenager, and Ethan's anger had soured the relationship for her. Now she could see that it had all been a façade to protect himself and she understood why it had been necessary.

She'd done the same thing when her mom had told them she was leaving. When you knew the heartache was coming and there wasn't a darn thing to be done about it, choosing to pretend it didn't matter was somehow easier.

She smiled. "I learn something new about you all the time, Sheriff. When I get Big Red home, I promise I'll make room for us. To see where we can go from here."

He kissed her forehead and took her hand. "Then we better get that cat of yours found, pronto."

Feeling like a teenager again, Maddie squeezed his hand and they returned to Maple Lane, where the twins and Angel were eating ice-cream outside the community center.

"Laura got a call and had to go, but we managed to put up all the posters first."

Angel gave her a knowing glance, and Maddie released Ethan's hand.

"Thanks everyone for your help today. If there's any way I can repay you, let me know."

"Cookies," Jessie said.

"Cookies," James repeated.

"Doughnuts." Angel winked.

Maddie laughed. "Nothing for you, Sheriff?"

Ethan was straight-faced as he delivered his answer. "I think we both know what I want."

Her cheeks flamed, but Maddie merely smiled. "Then I better get home and start baking."

Chapter Nine

Maddie drove through the quiet streets in her beloved Honey, the jeep her grandfather had bought for her when she was still in high school. With the top down and the sweetness of mown grass adding to this small bliss, Maddie had time to ponder the events of the last couple of days.

It had been a roller coaster with everything that had been happening and she'd felt the need to stop by Jed Clayton's, so he knew she, as well as Gran, was treating Sissy's disappearance as importantly as Big Reds.

She'd made a batch of cookies after Ethan walked them home to bring him. He waved and came down off his porch when he saw her.

"Maddie, how's it going. Have you any news?"

Hope hung on him like a bright light, and she flinched at the idea of snuffing it out. There was no way to sugar coat her answer.

"No news, I'm sorry. What about you?"

His face crumpled like a lump of dough with the air punched out of it and Maddie felt like she'd kicked a puppy.

"Nothing at all. I'm so worried." His eyes filled with tears.

Maddie put an arm around thin shoulder. A tall man with a proud bearing, Gran's friend, who prior to this had always looked younger than his more than seventy years, had begun to look his age. He even had the appearance of a slight stoop now. It tugged at her heart and added to the worry for Sissy and Big Red.

"I can empathize with thinking that you're not doing enough.

He sighed. "It's just that it's been so long. I've read things about the first few hours being the most important." He wiped his face with a handkerchief. "How long has Big Red been missing?"

"It's been a few days." She couldn't help the quiver in her voice.

Jed looked anxious. "I hear the spate of other dogs and cats going missing in and outside Maple Falls is continuing."

"Me too."

"What do you think it means?"

She had to say something to ease his worry. "The sheriff has an interesting theory that someone's got a list of breeds and they're taking animals from wherever they can to fulfil it."

His eyes widened. "And selling them?"

"Exactly. Which could mean the animals would be taken care of and are safe," she said as encouragingly as she could.

His eyes filled with tears and she hugged him, wishing he had family to get him through this.

He blew his nose loudly in her ear. "As bad as I feel about Sissy being missing, that does make me feel a little better. But if that's the reason they're being snatched, why would they take Big Red?"

Maddie took a step back. "Sorry?"

"Of all the animals they could take, he's not exactly a pedigree or a spring chicken, is he?"

She was outraged on Big Red's behalf but had been brought up to respect her elders. Plus, Jed Clayton wouldn't be trying to upset her intentionally. He didn't have a mean bone in his body.

"I concede he's not young. Then again, he's not that old. And he's a good-looking boy."

He nodded. "That's true." Glancing up and down the street he lowered his voice. "They'll be safe, won't they?"

It was a plea and Maddie's throat tightened. "I'm counting on it."

She felt so sorry for him and couldn't help thinking that they should have heard something by now. If Big Red had been stolen, by the same person or persons who stole Sissy and the others, then why wouldn't there be a ransom note? And what about all those other owners. Had they received notes but were listening to the petnapper and keeping it to themselves in the hope of getting their pets back?

Poor Jed. He was totally bewildered by everything, and Maddie wasn't any clearer. Goodness knows what state she'd be in if Big Red didn't show up soon. It didn't bear thinking about, so she told him of an idea she'd come up with while baking.

"I've decided to put up a reward. I'll make new flyers this afternoon, offering one hundred dollars for leads that result in the safe return of Big Red. Perhaps you'd like to pool our resources and add a little something?"

He gave it some thought, managing a small smile. "You've had that cat since you were a teenager. I remember how he used to follow you everywhere. He got himself into quite a bit of trouble at the college too, didn't he?"

A lump caught in her throat at the memory, but at least the reminiscing seemed to be doing him some good.

"That's right. He didn't understand pets weren't allowed. He's always assumed he could go where he pleased. Thanks for reminding me, it makes me hopeful that they both simply got lost and will be home soon."

His eyes cleared. "I think pooling our resources is a great idea. Put me down for one hundred too. I don't think it will hurt and might make the kidnapper show his hand."

Maddie was glad to see some of Jed's fight returning. "Great. I thought I'd try to contact some of the people missing pets and see if they'd also contribute. As well as offering a larger reward, we could do some extensive advertising in the surrounding areas."

His smile grew. "I can see this is in good hands. Good luck with the donations, and please tell me if you find out anything. Anything at all."

Maddie nodded. "You can count on it. I'll be in touch Mr. Clayton."

She walked quickly around the retirement community dropping flyers into letter boxes instead of hand delivering as planned, since she already had them made. Then she ran back to her car, already thinking of the wording for the new flyer.

As she drove, she saw the building that housed the local paper. It didn't serve a huge area and wasn't open today, but she'd be on their doorstep first chance she got tomorrow. A reward had been the best idea since the phone tree and she wanted to contact everyone who had a pet missing right away. Her heart was pumping and she had a surge of hope which sustained her until she got home and found her list.

Switching on the computer, she was soon typing out an advert for the paper and found another great picture of Big Red. It was different from the one she'd used on the flyer, where he was sitting in the doorway at Gran's, the sun shining on his red-blonde fur, looking like he owned the cottage and all he surveyed

In this one he was stretched out on the back of Gran's rocker. A precarious position for a cat his size when no one sat in the chair to keep it balanced. It was, however, safe-guarded by the fact it was close to the cottage wall, and so heavy it couldn't tip the wrong way. How he knew he was in no danger, was a mystery. The idea of him doing a few tests when no one was watching made her smile. He was, after all, a very clever cat.

Satisfied with her efforts, she walked down to Gran's for Sunday dinner. Now they didn't live together, it was especially nice that Gran had resurrected this weekly ritual from her childhood.

When Gran moved from the apartment above the shop she'd shared with Maddie for a few weeks, back to the cottage after deciding not to sell it, Maddie really missed having her around all over again. Still, it wasn't as bad as when they'd lived in different states, and New York City had been a little far to come for a home cooked meal, no matter how good.

Laura moving into the cottage helped to fill the Maddie void, so Gran said. Plus, it was nice for Laura to share in their small family rituals, since her own was family relation-ships were so awful. Not that Maddie knew Laura's parents, but she'd heard enough about them from Angel to form the conclusion that they didn't appreciate what a wonderful daughter they had.

Gran was waiting at the door, her floral apron looking as

pristine as it always did, regardless of the amount of cooking she'd done.

"Good timing, sweetheart. Dinners ready." She held open the screen door and they walked arm in arm down the wide hall to the kitchen where Laura was mixing something on the stove top.

"Hey, Maddie. Gran let me help with dinner, so don't blame her if it's not as good as usual."

"I have no fears. You're picking things up pretty quickly at the shop, so I'm sure you'll be doing the same here."

Laura blushed. "Thanks."

Maddie waved away their mutual embarrassment and helped set the table, glad to be with company. Dinner was more fun than she had anticipated, and a welcome distraction from fretting about Big Red every second.

"Want me to keep you company tonight?"

"I appreciate the offer, Laura, but I'll probably putter around until bedtime. If you'd like to come in early tomorrow, we can practice making bagels again?"

"That would be great. I'd like to improve so we can begin selling them."

Gran tutted. "You girls need to have some fun. You can't spend every minute baking."

Maddie snorted. "There's not much else to do. Maple Falls isn't exactly a hive of activity."

"What a lot of rubbish. You could go to O'Malleys for karaoke or quiz night."

Laura gaped at Gran, then Maddie, and they both burst into laughter.

"I don't think that's for us," Maddie said when she could.

"Why not? Or do you think you're too old for that kind of thing?"

Maddie was horrified. "Old? No way. The problem is, we're too young."

Gran sniffed. "It's not New York City, I grant you, but that just means anything going is for all ages. Besides, you both need a man in your lives."

Maddie dropped her fork, while Laura looked like a deer in headlights.

"There isn't a man within forty miles who's not married or already taken." Casually, Maddie picked up the fork and tried to eat.

Gran wasn't about to let the matter drop. "Now, that's simply not true. For a start there's Ethan, and his deputy, Robert. As far as I know neither are currently attached."

Maddie blamed her sleep deprivation for not seeing that coming. "I'm not interested and we're just friends."

"Our Sheriff has the hots for you something bad. And from what I see, you like him right back. When do you propose to do something about it?"

"Gran!"

Undeterred, her grandmother calmly brushed a few crumbs with the side of her hand into a pile beside her plate. "All I'm saying is that there are a lot of women hereabouts who are looking for a man like Ethan. If you're not careful, you'll find him snapped up. Then where will you be?"

"Right where I am now. Single and happy to be so." Maddie purposefully stacked the empty dessert plates. "I'm doing the dishes. You should stay here and annoy Laura with your ideas for a boyfriend that would suit her." She winked at Laura, who responded by wrinkling her nose. Maddie, artfully dodging further conversation on the subject, took the plates to the kitchen and left them to it.

Gran had always been deeply fond of Ethan, and when

Maddie first returned she'd wondered how long it would be before her grandmother started pushing them to rekindle their relationship from the past. Apparently, her reprieve was over.

Looking out from the kitchen window, as the light bled from the sky in a red-streaked pattern over vast fields, Maddie felt the melancholy start to descend once more. Laura came to help dry the dishes but didn't say much. Perhaps this was due to Maddie's worry, or maybe Gran had given her food for thought. Laura had harbored feelings for Ethan and knew Maddie was aware of them. This made them both a little awkward around the subject.

"Thanks for your help today," she broke the silence.

Laura came back to her own thoughts with a start.

"It was nothing. I hope tomorrow will bring a good result."

"Me too." Maddie crossed her fingers and Laura did the same.

With the kitchen tidy and Gran happily ensconced in a floral, wing-backed chair with her knitting, she walked home, glad to have spent the evening with them despite Gran's matchmaking attempt.

Chapter Ten

Maddie jumped out of bed on Monday, not because she had to, it wasn't yet 5am after all. No, she'd had a dream Big Red was nearby and calling her. She raced downstairs and wrenched open the kitchen door.

Of course he wasn't there, but her heart sank anyway. This was torture and becoming a struggle to hold herself together. Slowly, she turned the range on and went upstairs for a shower and to dress.

An hour later Laura arrived. She didn't look her usual, perky self.

"You didn't get a good night's sleep either?" Maddie asked.

"Not the best. What are we baking today?"

Laura didn't seem to want to talk about whatever was bothering her, so Maddie let her be. Once they were baking and in the zone, the chatting began as usual.

"I'm so glad that our new employee is starting today."

Laura frowned, apparently having forgotten. This was odd when she'd been so excited last week by the news.

"Of course. Luke, you said? I'm looking forward to not being the new kid on the block anymore."

Maddie laughed. "If he's as quick to learn as you, I'll be delighted." She gave Laura a thoughtful look as an idea popped into her head, as they had a habit of doing. "Actually, I've managed to get a bit done already this morning and I'd love to drop off more flyers sometime during the day. But only if you two have things under control. Although, with it being his first day, it might be a bit much to ask."

Laura smiled gently. "I'm sorry Big Red still isn't home yet, and you should totally get more flyers out there. Go whenever you want. Besides, you deserve some time off and I know it will make you feel better."

Maddie smiled. "It's Monday. I've had plenty of time off, but you're right, I'll feel better doing something proactive about it. Let's get going with the bagels and see how the day goes, and I promise it won't be over lunchtime."

"That's a relief. It's crazy most days at that time of day, but I won't tell the new kid that."

They grinned at each other, and Maddie felt a genuine warmth flow through her. Finding a friend out of their tenuous earlier relationship was a huge bonus to having Laura work here.

A couple of hours later the display case was full. Laura made coffee to prepare them for the rush when there was a knock on the shop door. Maddie went through to find Luke Chisholm outside, a little early, which boded well. She let him in and left the door unlocked as it was nearly opening time. They always had a few early morning customers who had to have their coffee fix.

"Morning. Ready for your first day?"

Eyes bright, he nodded. "So ready. I couldn't wait for today and I hardly slept all weekend."

This was music to her ears. "Great. From now on come around the back and just walk in. we might not always hear you knocking if we're in the kitchen."

They walked through the shop to find Laura frosting a large chocolate cake.

"Wow. That looks great."

She grinned at him. "Hopefully we sell it before our friend Angel sees it. She loves cakes, and this one might be her favorite. I'm Laura." She apologetically held up her hands which were sticky with frosting, so she was unable to shake his.

"Yes, I know who you are. Our parents are friends and we met at your rally."

Laura paled. "Oh. I'm sorry, I don't remember you. The election is a distant blur to me. How did you come to be there?"

He shrugged. "You know how it is? My parents insisted we create a united front."

The conversation concerning the darker days of her life was all it took for Laura to shake a little and she took a seat at the counter. "I do know exactly how that works."

"Are you okay?" he asked.

"Sure. You must know, I'm not proud of the election or of my parent's behavior."

Luke nodded. "Our dads are in the same network. It's hard to be the child of parents who want more from you than you're prepared to give, in ways that don't sit well."

Laura gave a feeble smile. "You sound so much wiser than I was at your age." Then she frowned. "Do yours know you're working here?"

It was Luke's turn to look uncomfortable. "Well, I haven't exactly told my father yet."

A look of understanding flowed between Laura and

Luke, while Maddie had a sinking feeling. She'd watched the interchange with growing concern, knowing she had to address this right away.

She clasped her hands together. "I hoped you'd cleared it with your parents before you started, Luke. Is it going to be a problem when you do?" she asked.

The teenager straightened his shoulders. "Not as far as I'm concerned. I know what I want to do and I'm determined to do it. I'm old enough to make up my mind about what career path I want to take."

Maddie couldn't doubt his sincerity. She just hoped between him, Laura, and their assertive parents, she didn't lose all her staff anytime soon. The shop was getting busier every week and if it was just her and Gran again they wouldn't be able to cope.

And more than that, she loved watching Laura blossom as a baker and being happier every day. If Luke felt the same, she would be thrilled.

Just then the bell rang. It was still early and she was especially surprised to see this particular customer, who took a more leisurely approach to leaving the retirement community. Jed Clayton stood just inside the shop, his face pale.

"MM Maddie. . ."

She hurried to him and pulled out a chair. "Please sit down, Mr. Clayton. Laura, will you get a glass of water, please?" she called out.

It didn't take long before Laura handed her a glass. Maddie knelt if front of him and waited while he gulped down some water. He closed his eyes for a second, as he attempted to get himself under control.

"I practically ran all the way here because I didn't trust myself to drive. Thank goodness you were open."

Maddie had an image of him running and pursed her lips for a second. "What's happened that has you so worked up?"

"This." He pulled a wrinkled piece of paper out of his pocket and thrust it at her.

Maddie's heart sank, but she took it from his shaking hand as she willed hers to be firm. This scenario brought back memories of the threatening notes she had received not so long ago. She spread it out on the table and could see it was everything she feared.

'If you want to see your mutt again, you better leave five hundred dollars in an envelope in the park trash dumpster on Sunday morning. The one at the back, by the trees. Don't tell a soul, otherwise Sissy is a dead labradoodle.'

Maddie gasped and handed the note to Laura, all the while wondering if the dog thief had also taken Big Red and if the next letter would be for her.

She took a deep breath, not wanting to alarm Mr. Clayton any more than he was. "When did you get the note?"

"I'm not sure when it was put there. I went outside this morning to see if Sissy was back, and there it was. Her kennel is on the porch, even though she hardly used it. She was supposed to be an outside dog, but that didn't suit her." His eyes were misty as he spoke.

Maddie understood. Apart from Suzy's Pomeranian, Sissy was potentially the most spoiled dog in town, a fact she couldn't comment on since Big Red had a pretty easy life too.

"Where did you find it?"

"Attached to the front of her kennel with tape. It certainly wasn't there last night."

She frowned. "I'm guessing you didn't see anyone around?"

He shook his head. "Not last night and certainly not at this time of the morning. I'm an early riser, even if I don't have to be anywhere, and the world is a quiet place. Something you'd know all about, I daresay. I think it must have been left in the middle of the night."

"It is a little damp, which is probably from the dew we had."

Mr. Clayton nodded enthusiastically. "That was my guess."

She put her hand on his arm. "I think we should tell the Sheriff about this."

"But it says don't tell the police, which is why I came to you. I know how you solved the mayor's murder and thought you could help me without involving them. I couldn't bear anything to happen to my poor Sissy. Five hundred dollars is a lot of money, but I'll pay it if I must."

"I understand, but I learned my lesson about not trusting the sheriff. I promise he'll be discreet and will know better what to do about the ransom than I possibly could."

Nearly being killed still haunted her dreams from time to time and reminded her she was a baker and not a detective. Still, she couldn't ignore Mr. Claytons' call for help. Especially if whatever was going on here involved Big Red.

He nodded reluctantly, then grabbed her hand. "Don't bring the sheriff to my house in case I'm being watched. You talk to him elsewhere on my behalf and get his take on this."

"I'll call him right away and see if he can stop by here."

Maddie slipped her hand free and when he stood was relieved to see he was much steadier.

"I better get to the bank. I want to be there as soon as it

opens, so I have things ready just in case it's necessary to pay the ransom"

She wanted to lift his spirits and had hoped to talk him out of withdrawing his money right away, but his mood was still dark with fear and looked determined to complete his mission, regardless of anything she or Ethan might say.

"Please be careful about handling such a large amount of money, Mr. Clayton, just in case the person who sent the letter is waiting for you to get it. It could be an opportunist who heard about Sissy being missing and sees this as a way to take advantage of the situation."

He paled once more. "I hadn't thought about that. I'm so upset my brain won't work right."

"You're doing great. Why don't you stay for a cup of tea while I call the sheriff?"

He hesitated, but Maddie was truly worried that he was getting himself worked up. Deciding she wasn't taking no for an answer, she pushed him gently back down into the chair. He slumped, looking bewildered.

Maddie quickly made the tea and brought out the set on a tray. She could see how his hands shook and without asking poured the tea into a cup with green ivy around it. She had chosen this set in particular because green was the color of hope.

He sighed and closed his eyes as he sipped, while Maddie brought him a cheese scone on the matching side plate and a small dish of butter.

"I'm not hungry, dear."

He probably hadn't eaten anything this morning with all the stress and was still pale.

She frowned. "Don't make me get Gran. You need to eat, otherwise you won't have the strength to see this through. If you think about it, this is a good thing. At least you know she's safe. Right?"

Suddenly, he had a bit more life in him. "Yes. That's right. And she's coming home." He cut a small piece and popped it in his mouth. His smile said how much he enjoyed it, as did the way he spread the butter and devoured the rest of the scone in record time, despite his earlier protestations of not being hungry.

While he finished his tea, Maddie went out to the kitchen and rang Ethan. There was no answer, so she left a message for him to call her back.

She was explaining this to Jed Clayton, when a harried looking Maude Oliver, burst inside. Her pale blue hair was all over the place, which was unheard of as president of the Country Club and leader of the blue brigade. Those women prided themselves on always having a perfect appearance. None more so than Maude.

"Whatever is the matter, Mrs. Oliver?"

The tall austere woman had the potential to scare even the hardiest of Maple Falls citizens, but right now she looked confused, and scared? Her eyes darted about warily, as she kept an eye on the door.

"Pardon?"

"I'm asking if you're okay. You look upset, and I wondered if I can help?"

Maude clasped a Gucci bag to her heaving chest, dragging in a ragged breath. "I've come in for a cup of tea not an inquisition," she said, as she peered out the window. "Plain. Not that fruity stuff."

Maddie's concern faded slightly. You couldn't help some people. That was a fact. "I'll get your tea right away."

Mr. Clayton gave her a sympathetic look as she passed

him, then went back to his tea, careful not to make eye contact with her other customer.

It was proving to be one of those days that were fraught with oddities. She went to the restaurant grade hot water dispenser and filled a pot to warm it. Choosing the set with blackberries on the side, since the prickles seemed appropriate, she took it through to Mrs. Oliver, who had sat at the table closest to the window.

She would have made conversation as she put everything in front of the woman, but Mrs. Oliver seemed barely aware of her. The woman absently pulled the tray closer, and as she poured tea her hand shook so badly that she then had to grasp the cup in both hands to get it to her lips.

Laura who had been frosting cookies in the kitchen, and was now putting them in the cabinet, raised her eyebrows at Maddie, who shrugged her shoulders. If Maude was friendlier she might be inclined to push, but past experiences told her that this member of the blue brigade would not take kindly to any more questions no matter how well-intentioned.

"I'll wait to hear from you, Maddie," called out Mr. Clayton as he left. He appeared to have a little more color but was clearly eager to get back to the matter at hand.

Maddie scooped up his money and cleaned down the table where he'd sat, noting that Mrs. Oliver's focus was on something or someone on Maple Lane. Sipping her tea, she also looked repeatedly at her watch. Perhaps she was meeting someone. Probably her good friend Irene Fitzgibbons, vice-president of the Country Club. They were often together.

Returning to the kitchen, she began to load the dishwasher when she heard Luke wishing their customer a good day. Clearly, she had misread things and Maude wasn't waiting for anyone.

Luke brought her dishes to the kitchen and instead of loading the dishwasher he placed them on the bench and fetched his bag from the alcove. Pulling out his wallet, he counted out some money. With slightly pink cheeks, he handed this to Maddie.

She allowed her staff to help themselves to drink or food during the day without charge, therefore this was unexpected.

"What's the money for?"

Luke looked like he wanted the floor to swallow him.

"Ahhh. I didn't get that lady to pay for her tea, so I'd like to pay for her."

Maddie folded her arms. She liked to be charitable, but as it happened, she knew that Maude Oliver was very comfortable financially.

"And why didn't she?"

Luke bounced on his heels. "She seemed so upset. I don't know what the matter was, but she wasn't looking right so I didn't like to ask her for the money when she got up to leave. I really don't mind paying."

Maddie felt her heart swell. "Well, it's very kind of you Luke, but I don't think you can sustain that attitude if more of our customers go down that road. Sometimes, people need a gentle reminder."

He shook his head firmly. "I promise it won't become a habit."

"I'm glad to hear it." She smiled. "I'm proud of you for being so kind to one of our customers. I'm sure she'll be mortified when she remembers and will make amends. Please, keep your money."

The relief on his face that she wasn't angry with him,

almost made her laugh. She was pretty sure she wasn't a horrible boss, despite what people said about chefs.

Luke shook his head. "Oh no, I couldn't let you pay for my mistake."

Maddie put her hands on her aproned hips. "I thought we decided it wasn't a mistake. Anyway, who's the boss here?"

"You," he said with conviction, looking uncertain as to how this was going.

Now she grinned at him. "Put your money away and I'm sorry for teasing you. I'll try not to do it too much, but I can't promise."

His eyes widened, then he laughed, stuffing the money back in his wallet, while Maddie wondered how she got so lucky. First with Laura and now Luke. Honesty was a big thing to Gran and naturally that had rubbed off on her. To find the same convictions in her new employee was a blessing she wasn't likely to take for granted, but good to know so early on. And good to see the kind of man he was.

Her phone rang and when she picked it up Ethan's name flashed up at her. Before she answered, she took it out into the garden. She trusted Laura and Luke, but she didn't want them worried unnecessarily and out here she could speak freely.

When she explained what had happened with Mr. Clayton, he said he would come by as soon as he could. He might be only coming to talk about the petnapping, but she knew she would feel a whole lot better getting the details off her chest. She had to admit, it came with the bonus of simply having Ethan nearby. Recently she began to realize that his presence gave her strength, in a similar way to Gran and her friends. Which couldn't be a bad thing.

Chapter Eleven

Understandably, Ethan arrived too late to speak to Mr. Clayton, but he was just in time for the next round of customers. Except they weren't customers and weren't at all happy.

Maddie felt as though she should have been prepared for this eventuality, yet the confrontation turned out to be a rude shock.

She'd made coffee for Ethan, and had just finished telling him about the petnapping, when the doorbell sounded followed by heavy steps and an angry retort.

"It's true then? You've quit college?"

Uh-oh, she mouthed to Ethan as she went to stand by the opening into the shop. She could see Luke behind the counter. The poor boy was pale, his knuckles white as he clenched them at his sides. Giving an apologetic look to Ethan, she went to offer Luke support should it be required. It looked like it was.

"Hello there. Everything okay?" she asked breezily.

A solid man who was as fair as Luke was dark, stood with his hands on his hips leaning towards his son. By their features there was no mistaking their kinship, although with his face an ugly shade of red, and taller by a good foot, he was missing the pleasant demeanor of his son. Behind stood a younger version, but she guessed that Luke's brother would be a few years older than he was. They glared at her, then Luke's father stood back giving her the once over, which was laced with hostility.

"So, you are the famous baker who coerced my son to give up his studies and his football career to make sales and bake bread?"

Maddie raised her eyebrows at the heat in his words. "I can assure you I did no such thing. Although, in the short time I've known him, I am confident that Luke's enthusiasm will ensure he does well. I'll teach him all I can and help him with whatever he needs to do to be successful."

"With the education he's had, my son can do a lot better than this." He opened his arms to encompass her store. "You're ruining his life."

"Dad, Ms. Flynn had no idea I hadn't finished college."

Mr. Chisholm glared at his son. "So, you lied to everyone?" Then he focused once more on Maddie. "You really want a liar working for you?"

Luke flinched, and Maddie was angrier for him than for herself. "I confess, Mr. Chisholm, that I don't know your son well, but he seems to me to be kind, honest, and a hard worker. That's all I need to know to give him a chance."

"A chance? To be a baker?" He gave a sneering laugh.

Ethan chose that moment to come through into the shop, startling Luke's father. It was a massive relief to have him by her side and that she had no other customers.

"Mr. Chisholm." He nodded at the confused man, then smiled at Maddie. "Since Ms. Flynn has won many prestigious awards, I'd say that she'd be the best person to know if Luke is cut out for a job like this. Wouldn't you?'

"Well . . .I . . . He should have finished college first. Like his brother, Johnny." He blustered nodding at his other son. Then he appeared to remember his own importance. "Regardless, he's my son and I should be the one to decide what he does with his future."

Ethan's pose was one of false relaxation. Maddie could see it but doubted Mr. Chisholm had a clue.

"Naturally, you might want some input. Although, didn't he turn eighteen recently?" As he spoke, Ethan had casually gone around the counter and was less than five feet from the men. Unconsciously, perhaps, they took a step back.

Luke's father obviously didn't like the idea of backing down and he stuck out his chest. "He did, but while he lives under my roof, he does what I say."

Perhaps he thought it made him look and sound tough, but Maddie, having had experience with men like Mr. Chisholm, thought him silly and pompous. Teenagers needed to have a goal that inspired them. The lucky ones found it sooner rather than later.

Luke, given courage by Ethan's interference, lifted his chin. "Then I'll have to leave home."

Mr. Chisholm slammed his fist down on the counter. "You will not!"

Maddie could see that Ethan was ready should this turn more violent. She sincerely hoped it wouldn't come to that sort of encounter. Fortunately, Luke, with a level headedness that belied his years, spoke in a calm voice as he attempted to talk his father down from his rage.

"Dad, if you can't support me in my career decision, then I'm sorry, I will have to move out."

The man wavered; his body still rigid with anger. His other son appeared to be in the same state, but there was something else at play here and Maddie couldn't read what it was.

A movement in the kitchen caught her eye. Laura was by the back door, her eyes wide with fear. With her own family situation not the best, it was inevitable that this loud showdown would scare her. Maddie wanted to go comfort her, but she couldn't leave Luke and Ethan to deal with the other Chisholms. Although, she doubted she could do much damage with a tray of eclairs.

Luckily, her baker's defense wasn't called for since Luke's father finally saw sense.

"You come home after work and we'll discuss this privately," he scowled at Luke. Then, ignoring Maddie and Ethan, stormed from the bakery, followed by the silent Johnny.

As he turned to face them, Luke seemed to shrink with embarrassment.

"I'm so sorry about that. Obviously, it would have gone a little better if I hadn't asked you to hire me until I finished college, but when I heard about the job, I knew everything else was a waste of my time. I saw your ad the first time, and I wanted to call you straight away, but I didn't. Then it was too late. When you advertised again, it was as if I was being handed a second chance. I remembered the sense of failure at not having the courage to go against my father."

He shook his head. "I guess I still don't have a heap of courage, but I'm learning, and this just proves that as far as he's concerned, it doesn't matter what I want. To be honest, I really don't believe the outcome would be any different whether I finished college or not. He would still have wanted me to go into his line of business. Working for Mr. Findlay in any capacity is something I have no interest in."

Maddie had never heard such passion and frustration from anyone.

Laura came out from the kitchen with tears in her eyes. "You did the right thing, Luke. Even people we love can be bullies. We don't have to stop loving them, but there is no law to say we must like them or be their victims. Well done."

He gave her an adoring look and stepped readily into her outstretched arms for a hug. It was the sweetest, most awkward thing Maddie had ever seen. She could feel her eyes prickle, and fortunately Ethan chose that moment to cough. Or, was it a deliberate ruse to dial back the emotion?

"Never let it be said that there's ever a dull moment at Maple Lane Bakery," she said gently.

Luke and Laura gave nervous laughs and Maddie couldn't help blurting out an idea, as she did when her heart was full of love and desire to help.

"If you need a place to stay, I can offer you a room here until you can afford a place of your own."

His eyes widened and she thought he might cry, but he took a deep breath and gave her a watery grin instead.

"Thank you, Ms. Flynn. I'd be grateful and I promise to repay you when I get some money."

She flapped her apron at him. "We'll worry about that later. At least you'll never be late." She just hoped she wouldn't regret her decision because living and working together could be difficult. *Too late now.* "And, by the way, my name is Maddie, and Gran, who you haven't met yet, is just Gran."

He nodded. "Okay," he said, not sounding convinced.

"We'll be side by side most days, and I don't answer to anything else."

He grinned at her insistence, and Maddie could see that he was already getting a handle on her teasing. She had such a good feeling about him and hoped for his sake that his family would come around to the idea of him being a baker. She simply didn't get his father's attitude. Then again, she had no children if you didn't count Big Red, but still...

Thankfully, she did have Gran, who would move heaven and earth to make her happy.

Chapter Twelve

Having had a meeting and a birthday party at the community center that day, Gran called by the bakery, while Maddie was out, to meet Luke. She told Laura that she was expecting Maddie for dinner again, because she wanted to hear all the gossip first-hand, and wouldn't take no for an answer.

Not feeling up to cooking for herself, Maddie was happy to succumb. The whole day had been crazy. From the ransom letter to Mrs. Oliver's bizarre behavior, then Luke's father showing up, it had been one drama after another.

As she got to the door, a sudden downpour hit. She hoped it would be over by the time she left.

"Luke seems a pleasant young man," Gran commented, once Maddie was settled at the table. "Is he a good worker?"

"He really is. Don't you agree, Laura?"

"I do. He has lovely manners and is great with the customers. I won't be letting him near the coffee machine any time soon, but he seems to have the knack of the basics, and can already use the register like a pro."

95

"Well done on hiring him. Now if we can just do the same with that fluffy boy of yours, life will be grand."

Maddie grimaced. "I'm so pleased to have him, but I feel like I need to do more to find Big Red, and I'm worried about poor Sissy, Mr. Clayton, and even Mrs. Oliver."

"Darling, you and the Girlz are doing wonders. I'm sure Big Red will be found soon." Gran kissed her cheek on the way to the kitchen to help Laura bring in the meal "I'm also worried about Jed. He was totally preoccupied at the birthday party and kept hold of a small bag as if it held the Queen's jewels. And what's this about Maude?"

Maddie told her how agitated the woman had been, but not what Mr. Clayton might be carrying. Clearly, Laura hadn't said anything either.

"Poor Maude has always been highly strung. She'll no doubt be right as rain once she's gotten the bee out of her bonnet."

Gran had a way of making things seem plausible, without trivializing them, and Maddie decided to tell her about Luke's family, just in case they turned up when Gran was in the shop.

"The father sounds like a thoroughly nasty piece of work. I'm glad Ethan was there to protect you."

"It wasn't me that needed protecting."

"Still if the boy needs a roof, you send him my way. You have too much on your plate as it is."

Maddie snorted. "And you don't?"

Gran laughed. "We Flynn's like to keep busy, make no mistake," she told Laura.

"Hah! As if I couldn't tell."

Then Gran kept them amused with tales from the community center. Older people could be hilarious, as Maddie was now only too aware. Because of Gran's involvement, every one of her friends, of which there were many, stopped by the bakery several times a week. Often just to chat, but most times they couldn't resist a treat while they were there.

They were relaxing after a superb roast lamb dinner with all the trimmings, when there was a loud squeal of brakes. It sounded very close, which was particularly unusual. Apart from Gran's cottage and the block of four shops, Plum Place had very few houses as the right side of the street was farmland that merged into the park opposite Maddie's bakery. Running out to the porch they were too late to see anything except taillights in the distance.

"Hooligans, no doubt," Gran grumbled, and went inside to serve up peach cobbler.

"Do you want a hand with anything tonight?" Laura asked as they headed back to the table.

Maddie shook her head. "No, thanks. I'm actually exhausted, so I might try for an early night."

"I hear you. The trouble is as soon as my head hits the pillow, I'm wide awake."

"Really? Me too," Maddie commiserated.

Gran looked at them fondly, insisting on doing the dishes this time. "Off to bed you two and try and get some rest. You both have eyes as black as used teabags. Go dream of handsome sheriffs and deputies."

"No thank you. But I am off. I'll see you both in the morning." Maddie gave them both a peck on the cheek, noting how pleased Laura was to be included in this small act.

Thankful that the rain had cleared, Maddie slowly walked home. It was dark now, but not too dark down this side of Plum Place because of the security lights at the back of the library and shops. The smell of summer was still strong, from the fields on her right to the small gardens on her left. The recent rain had its own unique smell and the trees dripped musically.

The walk also gave her time to think about Ethan. Sometimes it was a good idea to take feelings from the box where they'd been figuratively stored and occasionally have a darn good look at them. She hadn't wanted to in this case because it was still a little painful.

When their relationship ended because of her moving to New York City, and his inability to accept that she had to go, Maddie thought that was it. Coming home and buying the shop meant she was staying put and suddenly Ethan was in her life again. What did it really mean?

They both had some history, which was understandable given the years apart. She'd had a steady boyfriend and Ethan by all accounts had his share of girlfriends. This wasn't a big deal. Apart from his affair with the late mayor. The relatively new knowledge still rankled, since Denise had been one of her friends. It probably shouldn't, but it did.

She wasn't the kind of woman who jumped from man to man and found it hard to accept that others did. Before she'd met Dalton, there had been no one since Ethan. As they'd only broken up a few months back, it didn't seem right to be thinking some of the things she was. Plus, there were so many women in town, and maybe in the county, who found him just as appealing. These were the things that held her back from a relationship with him. As well as losing their newly regained friendship.

As she got closer to her gate, she noticed a dark lump half on the curb and half on the verge. Annoyance destroyed the last of the happiness she'd gained from being with Gran and Laura. Sometimes out-of-towners dropped their rubbish, which was infuriating to the residents who prided themselves on a clean and tidy town. She walked over to it with no thoughts of anything more sinister. Until she saw that it wasn't rubbish after all.

It was a body!

All she could think while rooted to the spot was 'not again'. After being first on the scene at Denise's murder, she had never imagined that scenario being repeated. She gave herself a mental shake. What if this time the person was alive?

Maddie bent down to the body and gently turned it over. Maude Oliver. She felt sick as she checked for a pulse on the cold wrist. Nothing. Cold and clammy, despite the balmy night, she pulled out her phone and dialed the paramedics. What on earth was the woman doing out this way at this time of night? She lived clear across town, near the country club.

After giving the few details she knew, and sure they were on their way, she called Ethan. Having the Sheriff as a friend was a blessing at times like these. Times? Should there ever be any 'times' like these?

He answered groggily as if she had woken him, but it really wasn't that late. Perhaps he'd fallen asleep in front of the television the way she did. She shook her head to get back some focus

"Ethan. It's Maddie. Can you please come to my place?"

"Now? Sure. What's up?"

She took a gulp of air. "Another dead body, I'm afraid."

Chapter Thirteen

Following her announcement, the kind of silence followed that either signified some heavy-duty information digestion or a lewd phone call. The latter was a revolting phenomenon she'd experienced several times while living in New York City. Appreciating Ethan's struggle she waited, although, not as patiently as he might think. She squeezed the phone, which did nothing but hurt her fingers, as if that might force a reaction from him.

"You're not serious?" he finally answered.

She was trying to keep her feelings of panic in check and was relieved to hear a rustle and the jingle of keys in the background.

Her breath came out on a shaky whoosh. "Deadly, I'm afraid." He could have asked a million questions. Thank goodness he didn't.

"I'm on my way."

Maddie went inside and grabbed the flashlight she kept by the fuse box, turning on lights before she went back to the curb to wait with Maude Oliver, so the poor woman wouldn't be alone. The soft light from the kitchen behind them, and the brighter one from the flashlight were reassuring while she looked across the road to the semi-darkness of the fields opposite.

When Ethan screeched around the corner, followed by the paramedics she couldn't have been more pleased to see someone. He jumped out of his dark sedan, ran across the edge of the grass, and knelt beside them to see who it was.

"Mrs. Oliver?" He was naturally as surprised as she had been.

Maddie nodded, despite knowing the question was rhetorical, as the paramedics arrived.

"I can't believe this is happening again. Please don't tell me she was poisoned, Ethan."

He stood and gave her a funny look, then took her cold hands in his. "Go inside. We'll talk when I've finished here."

As much as she wanted to be in her apartment, pretending this horrendous thing hadn't occurred right outside her bakery, she couldn't. A hundred questions were racing around in her head. First, she needed to know that this had nothing to do with Denise's murder.

While the paramedics were attending to Mrs. Oliver, Maddie left the flashlight with Ethan and moved away to stand at her gate, not sure what to do or how to feel. It was surreal and yet reminiscent of what had happened not so long ago.

Ethan was taking pictures with his phone when his team arrived. One of them took more pictures, with a proper camera, while another placed tape around Mrs. Oliver, and a third began to run crime tape around the area, as per Ethan's instructions. It was a very large area, she noted.

From a distance, she'd seen this happen with the police

in New York City. It had been chilling, but impersonal. These things always happened to someone else. Until they didn't.

Finally, they put Mrs. Oliver into the ambulance and the paramedics took her away.

"I guess there wasn't any hurry," she said to Ethan as he approached.

He followed her gaze to where the ambulance had been. "I'm afraid not. They think she's been dead for some time. How are you holding up?"

She shivered. "Now I can't see her—a little better."

"Good. Here's your flashlight."

He was about to leave her again. Maddie frowned, not liking that idea just yet. "Where are you going?"

"I need to check the area to see what happened. I'll get a better look in the morning, but I don't want any evidence to be lost if it rains again."

The sky held no promise of rain, but that didn't mean it wouldn't. "Exactly what evidence?"

He raised an eyebrow. "Tire tracks for a start."

Maddie gasped. "She was run over?"

"It's a distinct possibility. I'll know more after the autopsy."

She gulped, not wanting to imagine how he knew that she'd been run over, but it was too late. A clear vision of it happening was already in her mind.

Fortunately, the lights from Ethan's and the deputies' cars, along with the flashlights, made the area much brighter. While they were there and with her kitchen lights shining, not to mention Ethan's large presence, she wasn't so afraid of the dark and who might be out there.

"I'll wait for you here."

"That's best. I want the crime scene to stay clean."

He didn't have to explain, nor did he insist she go inside. While she waited, Maddie wondered who could do such a despicable thing? As far as she knew, Ralph Findlay, Denise's murderer, was still in jail so it couldn't be him. Could it? Had he escaped and no one had thought to tell the sheriff?

She couldn't take that idea seriously. Ethan had his finger on the pulse of the town. Usually. She watched him search the grass, and when his deputies joined him, they walked up and down the road. The flashlights picked up a thick black mark and they followed this down the road towards Gran's, then back. After this, they came back to the edge of the grass where the tape, in lieu of the body, was.

For some time he studied the area, making notes on a pad. Another car arrived and a man walked over to Ethan. They shook hands and spoke, then did another circuit of the crime scene, with Ethan pointing in several places.

When they were done they made their way to her. Maddie was colder by now, but found watching him work fascinating.

Ethan introduced the man who wore a long black coat and a sober expression. He was a little shorter but much broader, than the Sheriff.

"This is Detective Jones. He'd like to ask a few questions."

Maddie shook the man's hand. "Shall we go inside?"

"You two go ahead. I'd like to take a look at something, but I won't be long."

Ethan followed Maddie into the kitchen. He watched out the window while she made coffee and she could see he was curious.

True to his word, the detective came in just as she was putting the mugs on the table.

"Please, have a seat."

They all sat at the table and sipped the coffee appreciatively. The detective had a notepad out and checked his facts with Ethan.

Suddenly there were footsteps on the steps and the door burst open. Gran and Laura came inside looking pale. Gran ignored Ethan and the detective, which was not like her.

"What's going on? Are you okay? We saw the lights from the sitting room and came as fast as we could. I asked a deputy who was injured, but he wouldn't say anything. I had the horrible thought it was you."

Maddie stole a look at Ethan, to see if she was allowed to give the information she knew, but he was explaining the visitors to the detective.

"I'm fine. It was Mrs. Oliver."

"Maude? Oh, my. What happened?"

Gran grasped the edge of the table and Maddie jumped up to help her to a chair, while Laura made tea.

"She might have been hit by a vehicle."

Gran gasped. "How terrible. Do you think it was the one we heard earlier?"

Ethan's head shot up so quickly Maddie wondered if he might get whiplash.

"You heard a car hit her?"

The detective had been watching the interchange introduced himself, then motioned for them all to take a seat.

"Now you all know what may have happened. Let's stay calm and answer some questions I have as best you can. Did you see the incident?"

He had a no-nonsense voice and Gran shook her head.

"No, I can't say that. We were all at the cottage. I live at the end of Plum Place, so we couldn't have seen much from there. But we did hear the screech of tires and raced outside to see what was going on. Whoever it was, had gone by the time we got to the porch. I caught a glimpse of tail lights, and I can't be sure, but I think it was a jeep. I daresay the girls have better eyesight."

"Is that what you saw?" he asked Maddie and Laura.

"That's exactly what happened, and I'm pretty sure it was a car, but not a tiny one. The lights were higher than that." Laura said.

Maddie felt stupid. "I must have been in shock, not to have remembered that. It's so obvious now."

Detective Jones looked up. "There aren't many obvious things about situations like this, so don't beat yourself up over it. When was the last time you saw Mrs. Oliver?"

"Today. She came into the bakery and was very upset about something."

"Did she say what was bothering her?"

"No. I asked, but she wouldn't talk about it and was so shaken she forgot to pay for her tea."

He tapped his pen on the notepad. "I will need proper statements from everyone, but it's a bit late now. Let's schedule that for tomorrow." Standing, he turned to Ethan. "I'll be back when it's light to search the area more closely, if you'd like to meet me here?"

"Of course," Ethan said.

Maddie got up to look out the window and had a strong sense of déjà vu as she crossed her arms. Everything looked as normal as it had an hour or so ago, but it didn't feel that way.

Ethan stood beside her. "Whose car is that?"

"What car?"

"Under that huge Maple. My deputies are running the plates, but it occurs to me that it could be Mrs. Oliver's?"

Maddie peered across the street. She hadn't noticed it

106

before, because it was a dark color and almost hidden by the drooping branches. "That does look like her little beetle."

He nodded. Suddenly, Ethan took hold of her arms. "Did you walk to Gran's for Sunday dinner?"

She was shocked by his forcefulness. "It would be silly to drive that short distance."

"You didn't take your car and leave it there?" He pressed.

She pulled her arms free. "Why are you so bothered about that?"

"Maddie, is Honey parked in your garage?"

Her heart began to flutter, and not in a good way. "I sure hope so. Why wouldn't she be?"

"I need to check something. Wait inside—all of you."

Maddie was confused by his attitude, as were Gran and Laura. What did her car have to do with anything? They huddled together by the door and he was soon back with a way too serious look on his face.

"She's gone. As I drove past earlier, I noticed the door open, but didn't register whether your car was in there or not, since it was just a glance."

Maddie jumped up and ran out to the garage. It wasn't that she didn't believe Ethan, but Honey was her pride and joy. She had to see for herself.

The garage door was certainly wide open and the space where Honey had lived for such a short time was empty. She had closed it after returning from the retirement community. Hadn't she?

Ethan had followed her, and she looked up at him. "She's really not there."

His eyebrow lifted. "I noticed."

She threw her hands out, not a sliver of amusement touching her. "Where would she be? Who would take

Honey? Even if the thief gave her a new coat of paint, she's pretty distinctive, and there's not another like her hereabouts. Everyone knows who she belongs to."

"Exactly."

"What does that mean?"

He shook his head. "It means there will be a reason that isn't clear to me yet, and can you please leave this to the professionals?"

Maddie knew he was referring to her need to get answers first-hand, and she wouldn't pretend otherwise. "First Big Red, now my car, and you want me to sit back and not do anything?"

He ran his hand through his hair. "Look, we don't know that the two are connected. This could be a coincidence or far more serious than…"

"More serious than Denise's murder?" She finished for him and there was a lengthy pause.

"Possibly," he eventually admitted. "Promise me you'll let me, my deputies, and the detective handle this?"

Maddie crossed her fingers behind her back. "I promise I won't interfere with your investigation."

He sighed again. "I guess that will have to do for now. But I will be watching you."

"I'm sure you have better things to do."

He ignored this. "Will you be okay on your own tonight?"

"I'll be fine."

Ethan looked at them all pointedly. "I'll see you in the morning." He left without waiting for a reply.

Maddie tuned to Gran and Laura. "You two should go as well."

"I don't know how we'll all sleep after this." Gran hesitated. "Are you sure you wouldn't like to come home for the night?"

She lifted her chin. "No one's going to scare me out of my bakery."

"Do you really think that's the plan," Laura asked.

"Whatever 'the plan' is, I don't much care for it."

Gran stood. "I can see there's no point in reiterating what Ethan said, but please be careful, sweetheart."

"Always."

Her grandmother raised an eyebrow, but didn't comment further, and soon she was alone.

Maple Falls-was the most peaceful town she knew. Until Denise's murder and then Big Red's disappearance. Now there was another murder. None of it made sense, and Maddie spent several moments wondering if she had stayed in New York City whether things might have been different.

Moving her large and faithful feline three times in as many months had undoubtedly been too much for him. She desperately wanted to believe he had wandered too far because of this. She didn't think so, but it was preferable to imagine him being fed and cared for by a nice family some-where, who had no idea that the woman he 'owned' desper-ately wanted him back, than the alternatives.

Making sure she locked up securely, she began to bake with a vengeance. Missing pets, a potential murder, and Honey's disappearance required busy hands to get her mind to quieten even a little. Baking was her go to for thinking and solving this mystery would take a great deal of that.

It promised to be a very long night.

Chapter Fourteen

On Tuesday, after the worst sleep possible, Maddie baked bread and buns. There were also brownies and cookies she'd made last night. She was greasing pans for the muffin mixture when Ethan arrived as promised.

In truth she'd hardly slept at all and wasn't going to be admitting any time soon that she kept a couple of lights on.

"I need to get out to the site again, but wanted to see if you were doing okay?"

"I'm hanging in there." She managed through a throat tight with tears. "Laura will be here soon."

"Good. I'm only down the path if you need me."

She nodded as he went to where his deputies were already huddled around the grass. From the kitchen window she could see over the wall to where Ethan was greeting the detective. Between them, they had notebooks, cameras, and tapes to measure distances. She knew Ethan had done this last night, but in the light of day it looked strangely more eerie, as they rechecked everything.

Despite being upset about Maude, she couldn't deny an

eagerness to hear their findings. Knowing Ethan wouldn't take too kindly to her being anywhere near the evidence just yet, if at all, she restrained herself from going out there.

With the muffins in the oven, Maddie was happy to see Laura when she arrived, just to have someone to talk to.

"Morning," Laura called out warily, as she put her bag in the small alcove where the office was and tied her apron. "Any more news? About anything?"

She must have skirted around the group outside and be as aware as Maddie that there would be plenty of questions coming their way.

"What're the police doing out there?" Luke asked as he followed Laura inside.

Laura let Maddie tell the story and they watched his eyes widen.

"I can't believe it! She was only in here yesterday and now she's dead! Do you think it was something to do with how upset she was? She looked like she might have a heart attack any minute. Oh, that's not what happened is it?"

Maddie shook her head, sadly, although, not for a minute wishing Maude Oliver had had a heart attack. "I have no idea if the two things are related. They could be, or it could have been a case of hit and run and not someone out to kill her. Either is bad, and I hope that Ethan finds the culprit quickly. With it happening right outside, it gives me an awful feeling of not being safe."

Laura looked upset. "Then you should come stay at the cottage. It's your real home after all."

"No way. Like I said, I'm staying put. At least until I get Big Red back."

"And Honey. Maddie's car," Laura added for Luke's benefit.

Luke was puzzled. "I knew you'd lost your cat, but what's wrong with your car?"

Maddie could only take so much concern, but it was no good pretending things were better than they were. She sighed, taking a seat at the counter. "She's gone from the garage. Someone must have taken her when I was at Grans' for dinner last night. How they knew I'd be out is a mystery. It wasn't Sunday, Monday dinner is rare, and we decide any other nights day-to-day."

That seemed to trouble him even more. Then again, he had his own issues to worry about. Luke hadn't moved in, which was fine with Maddie. Apparently, the family had a discussion to work out a compromise. He wasn't very forthcoming about the details, and she could see he was embarrassed when he'd told her.

Which didn't quell the feeling he was getting a lot of negative talk at home about his career choice, because she'd caught him looking worried several times. She'd mentioned it yesterday, but he'd given her a sunny smile, and said he was merely trying to retain all the information he'd been given. Which was totally plausible, yet Maddie had a sense that all was not as right as he made out.

She was touched when he brought her a glass of water, while Laura put the kettle on.

"I'm sorry Ms. Flynn. I know from how you talk about her, how much you love that car. Here I am, thinking I'm the only one with a hard life. Mine is a walk in the park, in comparison," he said.

She couldn't help smiling. "What happened to Maddie? Ms. Flynn sounds too old, or you're referring to Gran."

"Sorry, all this business this morning has me spinning."

"How is everything going at home? Are you sure, you don't need my spare room?"

She hadn't intended to bring it up, but he merely shook his head.

"It was so kind of you to offer. To be honest, I'd decided I would, but Dad talked me out of it. For Mom's sake, I needed to let him."

"He was awfully mad that day," Laura shuddered.

He dropped his head. "I know, and I'm sorry you had to witness it."

"So, he was fine when you got home?" Maddie asked

That made Luke laugh. "Let's just say that it wasn't the best scenario. Dad was waiting for me and we had a predictable argument. I was all set to leave when Mom arrived. They had some heated words with each other in another room, and whatever she said made him back down." He shrugged. "After that I had to stay."

"Are you okay about it?" Maddie pressed.

He gave a wry grin. "I'm going to try. My brother and father can make life miserable if they choose, but for now I'll put up with it just so they leave me alone about working here. It's a compromise. My mom's cool. You'd like her."

Maddie shared a smile with Laura when she placed a cup of tea in front of her. He was such a nice kid. She could tell by his up and down manner that his decision to stay at home was entirely based on his mother's happiness and that touched a chord with her.

His good humor and willingness to share were important too. In a small business like this, they needed to be there for each other. Working so closely every day, there was potential for upsets and annoyances, and even though it was early days, especially for Luke, Maddie trusted that they could make it work.

"I'm sure I would. And if you do need to move out in a

hurry, the offer stands. I should mention that Gran has also offered you a room."

He nodded, his emotions warring with each other on his face, no matter that he was trying to be blasé about his home life. It was time to get things moving before he really got upset.

Finishing her tea, she stood. "Right. If we're going to open on time, let's get the rest of the cookies and cakes made." She went to the board by the alcove. "I was up earlier than usual and since there are now four of us, I thought I would get a weekly schedule done, and also a daily schedule, so we each have our own tasks and allocated time for training."

Laura grinned. "I wondered how long it would take you to make some lists."

Maddie had to laugh. Lists were her thing after all, and she knew that Angel, Suzy, and Gran, would say the same thing. Laura had clearly seen enough evidence to form her own conclusions.

When the knock on the door came, their smiles evaporated like spun sugar on a hot day. Not that Maddie or the others had forgotten what was happening outside, but for a few moments they had managed to keep it at bay.

Ethan entered, his hat in his hands, looking sorry that his presence today wasn't around better circumstances.

"I'd say good morning, but it's probably not the best any of us have had. I'm going to be taking statements from everyone and I'm sorry, Maddie, you'll need to come down to the station. It's just the procedure. No need to be alarmed," he said to them all.

She nodded. "Unfortunately, I do remember how this works."

"Can I take you now?"

"No, I'll..." She had been about to say that she would drive there. She gulped. "I guess I will come with you. Can you give me five minutes?"

"Take as long as you need. I'll be out back when you're ready."

Chapter Fifteen

Maddie made sure that Laura and Luke could cope without Gran, before leaving with Ethan. They drove in silence. No doubt he was trying to piece this together just as she was. The difference was he undoubtedly had far more clues and she was curious to find out what they were.

Deputy Robert Jacobs was already in one of the interview rooms setting things up when Ethan led Maddie inside. He gave her a small smile as Detective Jones entered.

"I'm sorry you're in this situation again, Ms. Flynn. We'll try not to keep you too long, but you can appreciate that we have to be thorough."

She nodded, surprised he had reverted to formality. Then again, this was a murder investigation and he certainly was more pleasant than he had been during their last encounter over a dead body.

The Detective waited until she was settled and motioned for Ethan to leave. "It's come to my attention that you and Sheriff Tanner have some history, and since I'm heading this investigation, I'll also conduct the interview. I'm sure you understand?"

Talking to Ethan would naturally be easier, but she nodded.

"Good. Let's start at the beginning. Where were you last night when the alleged murder occurred?"

So, they were still not sure? The detective was thorough and pleasant, if cooler than Ethan or Rob. When she had given all the information she could think of, she thought she was done, only Detective Jones wasn't impressed with her alibi.

"There must be someone else who saw what happened last night. It's not that dark in Plum Place and your car is missing."

For a moment, Maddie was stunned. Surely she wasn't a suspect? "Did you talk to the residents of the other shops? The library was closed just like all the shops, so it would only be the people who live above them, like Angel, who may have seen or heard something."

He regarded his notes. "Ms. Broome wasn't at your grandmother's last night?"

"No, why do you ask?"

"Because her lights weren't on and she didn't come by like your grandmother and Ms. McKenzie."

"She was probably asleep."

"At 8:30? I can't imagine that. What makes even less sense, is why Mrs. Oliver was at your place."

Maddie was confused. "But she wasn't. I never saw her that night, until I found her body."

"It may have been earlier that she came by to see you. When you weren't home."

"What makes you think she came to see me?"

He placed several photos in front of her.

"There were footprints all the way to your door. She had dirt on her shoes from where she stood in the garden under your kitchen window."

Maddie gasped. "You think I killed her?"

He shook his head. "That's not what I'm saying."

"I think you were supposed to say 'no' right about there."

He looked up in surprise. "Unlike Sheriff Tanner, I don't know you, and someone committed a potential murder near your property. You can surely see why these questions are necessary?" He didn't wait for an answer. "So, I'm asking, did you kill Mrs. Oliver?"

She folded her arms. "No, Detective. I did not." When he put it like that, she even felt guilty, and she didn't like it one bit.

"Now that we have that out of the way, let's go over once more about what you did prior to going to your grand-mother's."

She glanced at Deputy Jacobs who was taking notes and trying not to look at the two of them. Letting out the breath she hadn't realized she'd been holding, she explained her day. It was difficult with him studying her so closely.

"Were you angry about the way Mrs. Oliver treated you?"

"Not especially. She's like that with everyone."

"Did she talk to anyone else?"

"No. Even my staff let her be."

"What about the day before?"

"Ethan, I mean Sheriff Tanner, Laura, Angel, and I handed out flyers and put up posters around town."

"And you spoke to Noah Jackson. Anyone else?"

It was nerve-wracking knowing he had so much information on her. "I visited Mr. Clayton, then I came home to make new flyers since I've decided to offer a reward."

He frowned. "What did you see him about?"

"I wanted to be sure he was okay. He's terribly upset about his dog and worried that me talking to the Sheriff might have jeopardized everything, since he hadn't received his ransom note at that stage. He'll be even more upset when he finds out about Mrs. Oliver."

"Were they friends?"

"I shouldn't think so. She wasn't a favorite around the community center because they felt like she looked down on them. The Country Club group can be a bit uppity according to Gran. Still, she didn't deserve to die like that, and Jed will no doubt think everything that's happening is somehow tied to Sissy's disappearance." She frowned as a thought occurred to her. "I wonder if her dog turned up."

The detective and Rob exchanged looks, which intrigued Maddie. She had only been worried about the dog being fed, since its owner would not be coming home. Clearly, they had other ideas.

"I didn't know she'd lost a dog," Detective Jones said carefully.

Maddie raised an eyebrow. "It was reported, along with all the other animals."

The deputy studied her oddly. "No, I don't think it was."

"I saw it in the paper," she said defensively.

"When?" The detective pressed.

"I looked online the other day. It was an older article from last week. It really was there."

"That's very interesting. We'll check it out."

"You don't sound convinced."

"Right now, we're looking for a reason that Mrs. Oliver would be at your place at that time of night when you don't have anything to do with her outside of her being a customer of yours."

When said aloud it made about as much sense as chocolate frosting on a meat pie, and potentially put her as a suspect. Maddie felt the need to put things into perspective.

"An infrequent customer. One who had a missing pet and was terribly upset the last time I saw her. She kept looking out the window and up and down the street as if she were watching for something or someone."

"And you have no idea exactly who that was? Or why?"

"None at all. I tried to talk to her, but she bit my head off, drank her tea and left. Without paying."

"That doesn't sound like her. Maude Oliver always crossed her t's and dotted her I's." Rob said, then looked guilty for interrupting the interview. He shook his head at Maddie, who couldn't help a small snort.

The situation wasn't funny, but stress made a person's behavior a little off and Maddie was happy that the men had stopped looking at her like she was guilty of something.

"I agree. Not paying meant she was deeply troubled," she added.

Detective Jones stood, scraping his chair on the floor. "I think that will do for now."

He opened the door

Ethan entered right away. "If you're done, I'll take you back home."

Rob Jacobs flicked off the recorder and with a curious gaze at the two of them left the room with the detective.

"I could walk if you're busy?"

"I'm not too busy. Besides, I'd like to take another look around."

"Whatever for?'

"Sometimes you only see the obvious the first or second time around. Often, when you've taken a little distance from the problem things can seem a bit clearer or take you down another path altogether."

He sounded like a different person when he was in sheriff mode. Not at all like the Ethan she knew. Certainly nothing like the young man she'd left behind all those years ago, when they had been teenagers in love.

It wasn't a long drive and when they got inside, Gran, Laura, and Luke stopped what they were doing, eagerly waiting for information. Ethan wasn't interested in sharing any and gave her no time to do so either.

"Can you show me where Mrs. Oliver was sitting and where exactly she was looking?"

Maddie sat down on the chair close to the window. From here Maddie noted that the main street could be viewed quite a long way in either direction.

"This is it. You can see that she had a lot to look at, but nothing she wouldn't have seen a hundred times or more."

They swapped places.

Ethan looked up and down the street as she'd suggested, then he stood and turned to face the room, which he studied for some time. Maddie kept still while he worked, watching closely, trying to see things through his eyes.

"What's that?" he asked, pointing at the small pot plant which sat in the middle of the table.

"It's a cactus. All the tables have them."

"Not one like this," he said, pulling a pen from his pocket and scooping a crushed piece of paper from the earth. He put it down on the table and spread it out using the pen.

Bring the money to the green tonight. Five hundred dollars. Small bills. Don't be late and don't tell anyone if you want to see your crazy dog alive.

Maddie gripped the back of the chair. "Oh, my gosh. Another ransom note. Sitting there all this time."

"We don't know for sure that it was left by Mrs. Oliver."

She put her hands on her hips. "We do know it. She sat here. She was upset. Her dog is missing."

"And that still makes it circumstantial."

"You can't be serious?"

"I am. That's the way the law works. You have to be certain before you can say something is the way you think. Even assuming that she left the note, it doesn't help us know who is taking the pets."

She bit her lip. He was right. At this moment in time the note proved nothing. She walked through the shop and grabbed her backpack with the new flyers.

Ethan followed her. "Where are you going?"

"To do something positive. I can't sit here wondering. I can do that just as easily while I walk. If you've finished with me?"

"I can't think of anything else right now, and I can't stop you, but don't take any risks. This is not just about someone wanting money anymore."

The others were still waiting, and when Ethan said goodbye, they barely responded. It was nice that he was worried, but she'd told the truth. If Maddie stayed here to dwell on all that had happened, she might have a meltdown.

"Gran, can I take some of these cookies you've just made, if they're not for an order?"

"Of course, but I hope you're taking into account what Ethan said."

Maddie tried to erase the concerned expression with a hug. "I'm just going for a walk, and I might drop in to the station with these cookies for Ethan and his deputies for being so kind."

She didn't miss the looks the three of them gave each other and she sighed, leaving them to their suppositions.

Chapter Sixteen

Maddie's heart was in her throat as she came across another of her posters in tatters. Every single one of them were vandalized to the point of being unreadable. One or two might have been a coincidence, but not all of them. Someone had targeted hers alone and walked miles to do it.

What did it mean? That the person who took Big Red had killed him? She felt ill. Then she became angry. If this was a joke it was in bad taste, even if it was a child. Which she doubted, since the posters covered a fair bit of territory. Unless there was a group of petnappers. If it was a cat killer, or any other animal, then she wouldn't rest until they were behind bars.

Hurrying to the station she walked up to the counter. The woman behind it reminded her of the sloth from the children's movie, Zootopia, which Angel had made her watch a few weeks ago. Maddie did not recognize her, and apart from a finger in the air, as she continued to peck at her computer, it took a few minutes to be acknowledged properly. By this time Maddie was tapping her fingers on her thighs in irritation. The deputy might be new here, but that didn't mean she could be rude.

Eventually, she looked up. "Can I help you, ma'am?"

"Yes, please. Is Ethan available?"

"You mean Sheriff Tanner?" she said coolly. "I'm afraid that he isn't. Can I assist you?"

To be fair Ethan hadn't said he would be coming back to the station, and he had a wide area to look after, so she tried not to take exception to the woman's attitude, or disbelieve her.

"I hope so. My cat has been missing for several days. I've put up posters all around town. Since yesterday, this happened." She placed one of the shredded posters on the desk.

The deputy barely glanced at the poster. "Have you tried the pound?"

Maddie felt the wave of anger which had previously been directed at the vandal, now concentrate on the uncaring woman in front of her who, having made the inane comment, went back to her computer.

She read the name tag pinned to an ample bosom. "I can assure you that I've tried everywhere, Deputy Funnel. With the help of the caring members of our community, I have done everything I possibly can. With so many animals missing we need help from this department before more disappear."

The officer looked up annoyed at the further interruption. "We're busy with real crimes, ma'am. A missing cat doesn't really head the list right now."

Maddie was incensed. "Well, it should. Didn't you hear what I said? It's not one cat. It's several animals. If this is allowed to continue, it could be a catastrophe for the pets and owners alike."

The woman suddenly laughed, her chins wobbling a little. "*Cat*astrophe—good one."

"I beg your pardon, Officer Funnel, this is not a laughing matter. What if this was your child we were talking about? How would you feel then?" Maddie's voice had risen a few octaves which stopped the woman mid-guffaw.

"You wouldn't be threatening me, would you?" She raised herself, glowering at Maddie over the desk.

"Certainly not. I'm trying to explain that Big Red is like my child."

The officer frowned. "Yet, it's not a child, is it?"

"No, but..."

"Tell you what I'll do. Leave me a poster and I'll make sure all our staff sees it. Other than that, I'm not able to help further." Dismissively, she went back to her paperwork

Maddie sniffed. "I guess that will have to do. For now."

She was out the door before she remembered the container of chocolate chip cookies in her hand she'd intended to leave there. Looking back at the building she had spent more than enough time in lately, she decided she'd rather give them to Layla at the doctor's office than go back inside and deal with that woman.

Walking briskly down the street she tried to get her emotions under control. Did Ethan know he was working with such a heartless person?

Layla Dixon was a nurse and single mother to Jessie and James. Working long hours, Layla was a glass half-full kind of person, much like her brother, Ethan. Sitting behind the receptionist desk, squinting at the screen in front of her, she grimaced apologetically.

"One moment, please Maddie. Oh, this darn thing!" she dropped the mouse in disgust. "Spreadsheets! Sorry about that. Did you need an appointment? Grace is off sick today, so you'll have to bear with me if that's the case."

"I don't need to see the doctor." The way she said it must have alerted Layla to Maddie's mood.

"Big Red isn't home yet?"

She swallowed hard. "No."

Layla gave her a sympathetic look, as she came around the desk to hug her. "Hopefully soon. I'm glad you stopped by. I wanted to tell you that the boys had a wonderful morning with you, Laura, and Angel, on Sunday."

Maddie nodded and handed her the container. "They were wonderful to help the way they did. I brought you some cookies to take home to them."

"How sweet. They'll love them. Well, they love anything you bake as does the whole town. How's the cooking class going?"

"Really well. Nothing too arduous, but the girls are getting the hang of the basics."

"You'll be doing the diner out of customers, if they get too good at it."

Maddie grinned. "Hardly. I think this is a bit of fun for most of them, although Laura uses it for practice, and Angel is very studious about every lesson."

"Hah! The only one who doesn't need to worry about what she eats. Sorry, I don't mean anything by that."

"It's true," Maddie laughed. "But you have nothing to worry about."

"Keeping this place functioning right and running around after my boys doesn't give food time to settle."

"Better the boys eat them, than me." Maddie told her.

"Lucky for me. I mean, the boys." She gave Maddie a wink. "If you start up a cooking class for the rest of us, put my name down for it first. The only effort I make is on weekends, and we're all heartily sick of food out of a packet in my house."

Maddie grinned. "I don't know when I'd have time to run another class, but I have had people ask me about it, so you never know."

Some patients had arrived and were looking enviously at the container. Layla saw their glances and quickly stowed it beneath the counter.

"No point in having to say no," she whispered.

Thanks to Layla, Maddie walked out into the sunshine in a better frame of mind. She would go back to the shop and pick up more posters to replace the defaced or missing ones.

Chapter Seventeen

E than turned up first thing the next morning. The pinched lines around his mouth were a dead give-away that he was one unhappy sheriff, although he was only pleasant and polite to her customers. Maddie suspected it was her visit to the police station that had brought about this visit and having time to think about it, was embarrassed by her melt-down.

He stood at the back of the bakery until the last customer was served. This took a while, as without exception, they wanted a chat with their Sheriff on the way out. Maddie was grateful for the time to find an explanation of what had happened. When they were finally alone he stepped up to the counter, hat in his hand. His ready smile absent, she was glad her staff weren't around.

"Hello, Sheriff. Would you care for a doughnut?" Her attempt to encourage his good nature with a dig at the police and their liking for doughnuts, followed with a big smile, fell flat. "Or anything else?"

He frowned. "I'm not here for the food, Maddie, as you well know."

"Coffee?" she asked, hopefully.

"I'm here because you threatened my deputy."

The hat was getting a severe twist at its brim and Maddie hoped he wouldn't do it permanent damage on account of her.

"Shouldn't that be an alleged threat?"

"Maddie," he warned.

His displeasure over the misunderstanding rankled. "It wasn't like that. I merely posed a question and she took it the wrong way. I'm sorry if I was over-zealous."

He sighed, but wasn't capitulating. "What part of not interfering did you not understand?"

Maddie's hands went to her hips. "How is it interfering to bring the attention of the department to the vandalizing of my posters? Big Red is still missing. He didn't get lost as your officer assumed, and there are several other animals also missing with their owners suffering as I am. Deputy Funnel, wasn't slightly interested. In fact, she had no idea the pet stealing was so extensive. You expect me to sit back and just let the days go by without doing anything, when this isn't being taken seriously by your staff?"

He ran his fingers through his hair. "You've done a lot to help, and getting a few people to make a larger reward was a brainwave."

She could see he was making an effort to hold his temper in check, and she tried to do the same. "And yet we don't have our pets back."

Ethan gave his hat a few more twists, then his face softened. "I get it, I really do, but you can't harass my staff."

Maddie sniffed. "Your staff should be more attentive and polite. How is it that the deputy didn't know about the pets?"

"I'm sure she does. Sometimes there are other priorities that take precedence. You know, murders and such."

"Which are obviously connected. Maude Oliver was murdered because she didn't pay the ransom."

"We don't know that for sure," he groaned.

"Of course that's what happened."

He ran his hand through his hair again, making it stand up in an odd way. "You are the most exasperating woman I know."

She sniffed again. "I'm sorry you think so, but we both know I'm not about to let this rest."

"Perhaps we should talk about it when you're not so upset."

"I'm more than upset." Her hands went to her hips. "I'm furious, because no one seems to be taking this seriously enough."

The bell chimed and Maddie froze behind the counter. Mickey Findlay walked in with a grin as large as a Cheshire cat. Until he saw Ethan. The grin which never quite reached his eyes slipped for a few seconds, then with an effort he got himself together.

"Hello there. How are you two?"

Maddie gave him her own false smile, ignoring the unsubtle innuendo. "Well, thank you, Mr. Findlay."

"You must call me Mickey. My friends all do."

Maddie couldn't think of a thing to say in answer which wouldn't sound childish. The mans' nephew was a convicted killer, and while she couldn't prove anything, Maddie couldn't believe Mickey hadn't had something to do with Denise's death.

"How's Ralph?" Ethan asked casually.

They were barely three feet from each other in an awkward triangle and Mickey's almost black eyes narrowed.

"My nephew is doing his penance and that's all I'm prepared to say about him. I wonder if I might have a private word with Maddie?" His voice ran the vocal range of stiffness to slippery smooth.

The last thing she wanted was to be alone with him. "You can say whatever you like in front of the Sheriff, Mr. Findlay."

For a moment he gave her a cold, hard glare, then glanced at Ethan and his demeanor changed once more. He was like a chameleon, but she could see that Ethan wasn't fooled.

"I'm sure our busy Sheriff isn't interested in my proposal and it's a shame that neither are you, since it would be to your benefit."

He was toying with her, and suddenly Maddie lost the fight with her temper. "Do you know where Big Red is?"

It was almost a shout, and Mickey took a step back. She had surprised not only him, but made herself jump at the outburst.

"Who, or what, is Big Red?"

Even he wasn't a good enough actor to manufacture puzzlement on that scale. She took a deep breath. "My cat is missing along with many other animals. You must have heard about it?"

He made a rude sound. "I have no idea about any cats going missing. This was purely a business opportunity."

Maddie threw her arms out wide. "I've got about all I can handle here, thank you."

He gave her another hard stare, but she didn't flinch.

Straightening his cuffs, he smiled. "Well, I can see you've made up your mind, so I won't keep you from your business. Have a good day."

They waited until he'd gone, then they both began to talk.

"Don't ever be alone with him."

"What do you think he wants?"

Ethan put up his hand. "Did you hear me? Do not get into any discussions with him outside of this shop."

"I don't take kindly to being ordered around, Sheriff. Besides, isn't he innocent of any crimes that we know of?" She knew she was pushing him, but seemed unable to stop.

"I'm not ordering you around." He ignored her disbelieving look. "You know I think he's as dangerous as you do. Proving it is not as easy. He's a slippery devil."

Maddie tapped her thigh as an idea hit her. "You don't suppose it has something to do with the election?"

"How do you mean?"

"I assume, since he's friends with Laura's parents that he would have endorsed her instead of Maude Oliver to try to get his ideas across with little opposition. When Laura refused to stand, he decided to put his hand up. Right?"

"I guess that's how it happened."

"He had no choice, in the time frame to come up with a different option. Maude wouldn't have been a push over. Mickey would know that."

"What does that have to do with you and a business opportunity?"

Her mind was whirring with reasons for Mickey to involve her in any business dealings. "I hear there's a party on Friday night at the Country Club, to start things off for the election. You know a meet and greet thing? I'm wondering if he wanted me to cater it. Or, he could be after a donation?"

"Maybe, and you wouldn't want to do either?"

Her fingers tapped on her thigh once more. "Not for all

135

the tea in China. Maude and her friends were particularly rude to me at the last spring festival, and after. I can't prove it but I suspect that they were instrumental in spreading the word that my apple pie was what poisoned Denise." Her eyes widened. "Imagine if they actually had to eat my food?"

He smiled at the idea.

"As for a donation, I'd sooner have anyone as Mayor before Mickey. Even, as much as it pains me, Maude Oliver."

"I can understand that, what with having been stalked by Mickey's nephew. But, getting back to steering clear of him. If he comes back to talk you, please make sure he doesn't corner you alone."

Maddie shuddered as she remembered how Ralph Willis had tied her up and threatened her. That blood line was decidedly tainted in her mind. "I'll do my best. Speaking of unwanted visits—Laura's already in panic mode with her parents about to descend. Just having them in town is enough to give her hives."

"I know. The last time they were here she was a mess. Standing in front of a group had her stuttering, and the parents were merciless in berating her afterwards. Say, where is she?"

"She had to go to the airport and pick them up."

"Ahhh. Poor Laura. I hope she'll be okay."

"She has all of us in her corner. If her parents treat her badly again, Gran will be on their case."

Ethan snorted at the idea, and suddenly they weren't battling anymore. Maddie felt a surge of relief. Not finding Big Red was turning her into a Jekyll and Hyde. One moment she was sad and the next furious and she couldn't say what would set her off either way.

136

Ethan was leaving when Luke arrived back from delivering a birthday cake and regarded Ethan warily.

"Everything okay?" Ethan asked.

"Yes, sir."

Ethan's mouth twitched. "See you around then."

"S-s-sure."

Maddie saw Ethan to the shop door, where she shrugged. "I guess the law can be a little daunting for a teenager," she said quietly.

He grinned. "Because I'm so scary?"

"Yeah, that's it." She grinned back.

Ethan was still laughing as he walked down Maple Lane to his car.

Chapter Eighteen

Gran stayed longer that afternoon, so Maddie could take time off to run errands, as Laura was busy with her parents all day.

Spending a few hours in Destiny, Maddie visited the newspaper office, getting proper copies of every article where an animal was reported missing. This gave her concrete dates and names to contact. She wanted to know when and why some people stopped looking for their pets.

It was closing time when she'd finished, and when she got back to Maple Falls she was too tired to think about cooking. She stopped by the diner, deciding to pick up one of Isaac Carter's delicious chicken casseroles for dinner. She had just ordered and was waiting for her meal, sipping a glass of water, when Angel walked in.

Maddie sighed at how amazing her friend still looked at the end of the day. Several pairs of eyes swiveled towards the door, joining in her unspoken appreciation. New makeup and a haircut for herself would be a top priority, if she didn't invest every spare minute when she wasn't at work searching for Big Red. She bit back a laugh. Who was she kidding? There was no way she could compete with Angel, and she didn't want to. Angel was, and deserved to be, special.

Despite the unpleasant childhood and awful marriage, or perhaps because of them, Angel had worked her butt off to open her salon and make it a success. She was always upbeat and encouraging, therefore, her shortened name of Angel had little to do with the way she looked, but was all the more appropriate.

Angel was surprised to see her sitting in the booth closest to the counter.

"Maddie? What are you doing here? I called in to see you this afternoon, but you'd gone to Destiny."

"If you have time, I'd like to tell you all about it." Maddie pointed to the seat next to hers and Angel didn't hesitate. Maddie lowered her voice, since the diner had plenty of customers, and told her what she'd been up to.

"This is good information. Are you sharing it with Ethan?"

"I will after I've collated it. I already told him what I'd read online, but I think having these random acts in some sort of order, chronological and otherwise, might make things a whole lot clearer and therefore more important. I hope."

"Show me when you're done?"

"Naturally. I'll work on it tonight."

"Wow, you're having a busy day."

"Which is good, because it keeps my mind occupied, and is why I'm treating myself to one of Isaac's meals."

Angel gave a sly grin. "I do it all the time. Saves me from my own bad cooking and washing burnt pots. Although, I've a had a few soup and scone nights."

Maddie laughed, because Angel wasn't joking on the

burnt pan front. Most of the whole town knew of her problem because she was constantly having to buy new ones.

"Good for you. What are you up to this weekend?"

"The usual. Saturday starts with an early yoga class at the park with Noah, followed by a session of Pilates. Then I've got a full day at the Salon."

Maddie knew for a fact that Angel would walk to the local park for the first and then on to Noah's fitness studio for the second. The Park was opposite the bakery, but Noah's studio was at least a mile away. Maddie felt exhausted just thinking about that, let alone a full day on her feet.

"Sounds like a long, tiring day."

"I sure will be glad by the time I get home to put my feet up. But I don't think it's any more than you do on a weekday. I see your light on in the bakery kitchen when I get up and I bet you've already done a couple of hours work by then?"

Maddie hadn't thought about how long she worked each day. She'd being doing it for years—since she was an intern. The idea that this meant she was a real baker, when it had become second nature, made her oddly happy. Not that she didn't get tired, but she was often in bed and asleep by nine, so it evened out.

She smiled. "I guess you're right, but I wouldn't have the energy to do those classes, regardless."

Angel grinned. "You get used to it, and it wouldn't hurt for you to have some fun that didn't revolve around cooking. Anyway, I could go out looking for Big Red after work, if you had a specific place that needed it?"

It was typical of Angel to offer help in any spare time she had, but she'd done so much already.

"No need. I think the town has been saturated with flyers—as long as they haven't been defaced again. But, talking about having fun, I was thinking about going to the Country Club this weekend. They're having some sort of meet and greet for the Mayoral race. It's invitation only though, so I need to speak to Laura about getting tickets."

Angel's mouth pursed for a moment. "What on earth for? You hate that kind of thing."

"I do, but they're the only untapped group of people who haven't been contacted about the missing animals. I want to know if any of them have lost pets other than Maude Oliver, and if so, have they received ransom notes?"

"Hmmm. I see your point. I'm sure Laura could help. She's bound to have to go if her parents are here."

"It must be awful to have had to do things that make her feel so uncomfortable. I wish her parents were kinder to her."

"Me too, but I am so happy that you and Laura are becoming good friends." Angel smiled.

"We already are. She's so focused and funny in her own way. I think she's going to be a great baker too."

"Listening to her talk about how much she's loving it, and bearing in mind she's learning from the best, I don't doubt it. Getting back to this party–if you manage to get tickets, I'm not sure what the dress code is. In fact, I've never stepped foot inside the Country Club. I hope they aren't rude to us."

Maddie raised an eyebrow. "Us?"

"Of course 'us'. We're a team, aren't we? You do know that Suzy's going?"

"No way."

"Way. She was in the salon yesterday, getting a cut, wondering if she could get out of it. This thing is so last minute, and I think her invite's due to being on the town council, but as she's the principal of our only school, that probably played a part in it. I wonder if Mickey thought he could get Suzy to do some work for his campaign. A person that's loved and respected like Suzy would have some sway."

Isaac placed her food on the counter. "Is that all, Maddie?"

She stood and put her money beside the take-out container. "Yes, thanks."

He frowned at Angel, as if he didn't recognize her.

"I assume you aren't in here buying anything?" He shook his head before she could answer and turned to Maddie. "I don't think Angel has bought a single thing from me since your bakery opened."

Angel looked injured. "I don't think that's true, Isaac. I usually get something every day."

"Tell me what the last thing was you bought here? I haven't seen you for more than a week."

"Oh. I... Actually, I can't remember," she answered guiltily.

Isaac folded his arms, but his eyes twinkled.

Maddie saw it, and although she knew he was teasing, a small part of her hoped it wasn't true. It wouldn't be fair. Isaac's food was wonderful and in a small town everyone deserved to have customers.

"If that's the case, then I'm sorry. I guess it's because Angel and I are neighbors."

"As opposed to being best friends? Or that you bake better than I ever could?"

Both women shifted awkwardly until he gave a big belly laugh.

"Maybe you could come by a little more often to make

up for it, even if you don't buy a thing, since you do attract customers. That goes for both of you."

"What do you mean?" Maddie frowned.

"Every time you come in my takings go up, and it's not that you buy a lot. I'm thinking the other customers see you here and decide that if you can stand my food then it can't be the worst thing in the world for them to eat it too. And every man in town wants to be where Angel is."

Maddie and Angel laughed along with him, although both were embarrassed.

"I'll have what she's having." Angel pointed to the container.

"You don't have to do that," he said.

"Actually, I do, since I came in to get my supper before I knew Maddie was here."

The tips of his ears turned pink. "Touché, and well played."

Maddie picked up her food and smiled at him. "I will stop by more often, and perhaps we could look at ways to promote each other in the future."

"I already do. When someone questions whether my apple pie is as good as yours or Grans, I tell them 'no, it's not'."

Maddie gasped. "You don't!"

"I do. No point in spinning a lie. Everybody will know it sooner or later. I figure it's a little bit of goodwill that you've already paid in advance."

Maddie snorted. "Without knowing. I'll be more deliberate about it from now on."

"And I'll spread my food requirements between the two of you. Except for coffee." Angel shrugged. "You can't compete with Laura."

He pulled a comical face. "Don't remind me. If I'd

known about her talents I would have snapped her up before Maddie had a chance."

"Lucky for me you didn't. I don't think I'd be doing as well without her."

Angel gave a knowing smile. "Things have a way of working out. Look at my new employee. If Maddie had hired her instead of Luke, I would be a wreck."

They tried to argue the fact that she could ever look like a wreck, but Angel, used to comments like this, refused to listen.

"You know we should all have flyers up in each other's windows promoting our stores. Have you seen the ones Maddie and I did about Big Red?"

"Yes, and I was impressed."

"Why don't we make up some for all of us?"

"Sounds good. Have you had any reaction to yours?" he nodded to his window where a picture of Big Red was visible to anyone entering the diner.

"Not a word. But they are everywhere, and we're doing other things, thanks to my team."

"You have a team?"

"Sure do. The usual ones - Angel, Suzy, Laura, and Gran."

"Ahhh. The Girlz are back in action then?"

Maddie laughed. "Gran's just an honorary member of the Girlz, and Laura is new to it, but yes, that's us."

"You could do a lot worse. That team will get you into every place in town including the Country Club." He winked.

She frowned. "You heard?"

"I have flappy ears, so I'm not gonna lie to you about that either. With Laura's parents being friends of Mickey Findlay, it makes perfect sense she would get an invite."

"The problem is I know she won't want to go."

"You'll persuade her. I hear tell she thinks you're the best thing since sliced bread."

Maddie was already thinking of a way to ask Laura, because she'd bet a batch of chocolate croissants that it wasn't going to be smooth sailing.

Chapter Nineteen

Thursday morning arrived, with no further clues to Big Red's whereabouts. When Maddie finished her usual prep work, she got out the ingredients for bagels. After some success, and with a little more practice she was feeling close to being ready to sell them. Laura and Luke seemed to be enjoying the challenge too.

Arriving at the same time, they had their aprons on and were checking the large whiteboard Maddie had recently put up outside her small office. It was easier to refer to than the paper schedules she had initially made. It outlined what they were to bake that day and each item was assigned to one of them.

Naturally, she had the hardest tasks and the most since she was a lot faster, but she knew that having a job designated would lead to everyone doing their very best. After they had completed their necessary work, there was time to practice other things. Which was the only way to perfect this craft.

"Bagels? Cool." Luke tapped the board.

Laura saw it a second later. "Yay! I really enjoyed mine

the other night. I think they'll do well when we start to sell them."

"I hope so, and we are a team now. If either of you have ideas, I'm only too happy to listen and go along with you, if and when I can."

They looked happy to hear this and later they made two batches of bagels in between stocking the shelves with the other goods they baked and serving. Eager to try them once they had cooled, Laura and Luke pronounced them perfect. Maddie knew they weren't, but they were darn close. These would be in the charity box that went out this afternoon.

She had given Luke the job of preparing it, and he seemed to take this small task very seriously.

Laura was frosting a birthday cake ready for picking up that afternoon, when Maddie got the courage to ask her about tickets for the Country Club meet and greet. She perched on a stool on the other side of the counter and her fingers immediately began their tapping.

Laura stopped mid-smoothing. "What's wrong? Have I messed it up?"

"It's lovely. I think you're ready for the decorating side of things too."

"Are you sure?" she asked nervously.

Maddie nodded. "Why not? If you make a mistake, we'll redo it. It's the only way to learn."

Laura beamed. "I'd be happy to try. I think I love this side of baking as much as anything. It feels really creative."

"Don't sound so surprised. Baking in all its forms is creative. This is just another aspect of it."

Laura worked on in silence for a little while, then her hand stilled again. "You look like you want to ask me something."

"Do I?" Maddie prided herself on keeping her feelings

off her face. It was a must when you had to deal with an awkward customer or delivery person.

"You're tapping. You do that when you're anxious, or want to say something."

Maddie looked down at her fingers and recognized the habit. She wondered how many other people had witnessed her doing this and why Gran hadn't mentioned it? Prior to moving away, she'd made Maddie aware of it, thereby enabling her to control it better.

She sighed. "You're right. I want to ask you a favor, and you're not going to like it."

"I'd do anything for you, or the bakery. You know that."

"Don't be too hasty. I heard that you have an invitation to the Country Club on Friday?"

"How on earth do you know about it? Was it Angel?" she shook her head "I guess it was a natural assumption, but it doesn't matter, because I'm not going."

"I heard it's a meet and greet for Mickey Findlay and Irene Fitzgibbons in their bid for mayor of Maple Falls."

"There's no secret about that."

"Unless you don't belong to the Country Club. Which I and many other residents of Maple Falls don't."

"I guess that's true. I hadn't given it any thought. Especially, since I'm not running." She smiled. "It's such a relief."

"Were your parents okay when you picked them up yesterday? You didn't say much about it."

Laura frowned at the question. "They were fairly typical. Dad couldn't get a word in, and Mom monopolized the conversation around what was good and bad about Maple Falls. She didn't say too much about the election, to be fair, except to mention that I was expected to front up on Friday night. I think they're both happy now that Mickey's running. Maude Oliver might have been a formidable opponent, but Irene Fitzgibbons isn't in the same league."

She ran a hand over her bun, smoothing it. "You know, I'm pretty sure that Mickey would have realized I wouldn't have any more success than last time and now he has the perfect opportunity to get what he wants with minimal fuss."

"I'm glad to hear you say so. I've been looking at the history of the last couple of elections. I believe he still wants the land that his brother-in-law, Mr. Willis, donated to the town. He's always wanted to develop there, and if he's elected he can do what he wants, because no one will be able to stand up to him."

"Denise said 'no' because the whole community benefits from holding all the festivals and market days on that land. I don't think Maude would have agreed to making it available, since it would have been highly contentious. Mickey thrives on being that way." Laura gasped. "Do you think that's why they were killed?"

"Even if it was, no one could prove Denise's murder had anything to do with Mickey. I'm betting the same applies to Maude. That being said, there are other things that he might be involved in."

Laura tilted her head. "I feel that you're taking me down this path for another reason. What does any of this have to do with me?"

"If you got tickets for both of us and Angel, to go on Friday, we could find out if any of the members are missing pets and if they've received ransom notes. If some are and they're paying, then this might never end. If not, you could ask to put up flyers. It's kind of a win-win."

"Not for me."

Maddie's heart sank, but she could see Laura was

adamant. "I understand. Feeling that way is totally reasonable."

Laura dabbed at the cake half-heartedly. "I knew you had something important to say. I absolutely want to help, but the memories about the last election are far too real. People said terrible things to my face. It went on for months and no matter that it's been a while, I still cringe when any of them come into the bakery."

"It was too much to ask, and I'm truly sorry I did." Maddie felt terrible for bringing it all back to Laura. "I wasn't in town when it happened, but Angel filled me in, and it sounds awful. Please forget I mentioned it. There are always other alternatives."

Laura sighed. "I don't think I can. The missing pets are the main topic of conversation around town right now. The mayoral race is definitely second on the list."

Maddie nodded. "It's only natural when it affects so many people."

Laura put down her spatula. "If you're asking, then it is a big deal. And I love that pompous cat of yours. I miss him."

Maddie smiled and stood, placing a hand on Laura's shoulder. "I know you do, and Gran says if you don't ask you never get, but seriously, don't give it another thought. I'll get you the piping bag and some colors. You've done a great job. This cake looks perfect and ready for you to decorate."

She could feel Laura's eyes on her back as she went to the walk-in pantry. The last thing she wanted was to cause her friend more stress. It wasn't an alien concept to Maddie that families had a member or members who weren't as nice as they should be. Her own mom left her behind when she wanted more from life. The difference was she'd had Gran.

Laura only had her friends, and Maddie wasn't being a good one to suggest doing something which would cause her pain.

No matter that they had left the conversation on a warm note, the atmosphere in the kitchen felt strained and the afternoon began to drag. Maddie was relieved when Angel and Suzy came by as they were closing.

"Any updates on the murder?" Suzy asked.

Maddie shook her head. "I haven't heard anything."

"Irene Fitzgibbons was in for her wash and blow wave. She was terribly upset about the murder and telling everyone that she and Maude Oliver were best friends, until Gary from the garage, who was in to pick up his special shampoo, informed her that she might be the number one suspect if that was the case. She back-pedaled faster than a cat being forced to have a bath," Angel said with puzzlement.

Suzy grinned. "Don't worry about it. Irene couldn't kill anyone, unless it was by talking them to death."

"We shouldn't joke about it." Angel paled.

"You're right. I can't pretend that Maude was a friend of mine, or that I particularly liked the woman, but she's dead and it's not right." Suzy gave her a pained look. "I'm sorry I couldn't come by sooner, but the Meeting dragged on this week, because of the chatter around Maude and the pets."

"It's all good. I know you spoke to Angel, and you rang a couple of times."

"Still, I wanted to be here for you. Is there anything I can do to help make life a little easier?"

"Thanks for asking. I've done all I can think of. I wish I could come up with something else." She pursed her lips to stop the quiver that threatened to explode into an unexpected bout of tears.

Suzy made a soothing noise. "I saw the ad in the paper too. The reward should definitely help."

"One hundred dollars wasn't a huge amount, but with Mr. Clayton's and the addition of a few others it might be enough to encourage people to keep a better look-out, or for them all to be returned. I sure hope so."

Suzy tucked her auburn curls behind her ears. "So, it's definitely kidnapping and ransom requests for all the pets?"

Ethan had asked her not to discuss the ransom letters and she had also promised Mr. Clayton that she wouldn't, which made her feel a little awkward since she shared everything with these women, and they knew almost as much as she did.

"Even though I haven't had a ransom note yet, I honestly believe it is the work of the same person. Big Red was here that morning, and I wasn't worried until it was dinner time. I searched everywhere I could think of. It's not like he's small enough to stay hidden somewhere near for this long. Someone should have seen him somewhere. Every day I walk the area, speaking to as many people as I can. After that, I call the shelter and the vet, who are probably sick to death of me."

"I still don't understand who would take him. Or why," Angel pondered.

Suzy gave her a stunned look which Angel was oblivious to, and Maddie remembered Jed Clayton asking the same question, looking just as vague. They were used to Angel's rose-colored glass view of the world and Suzy patiently explained.

"His breed is worth a lot of money. There are all sorts of unscrupulous people who buy stolen animals. They don't care where an animal came from if it's one they particularly want."

Angels' perfect eyebrows shot up. "You mean like car theft?"

"Exactly."

"But that's terrible. I've heard of it, but until now, I couldn't believe it was even a thing."

Despite her history, Angel's innocence never failed to amaze Maddie. "I did find his collar, remember? It was undone. Big Red is clever, but not that clever."

"At least if he was taken, that means he didn't get..." Laura gasped.

"Run over? Lost? I've pictured every scenario, believe me, but I don't think he's dead. Does it sound stupid to say that I think I'd feel something more than I do if that were the case?"

The group looked at her and each other, as if they couldn't decide if she was actually crazy or not.

Laura smiled. "I believe you."

Suzy shrugged. "Only you know the bond you have. If you say he's not dead, then it must be so. I was at the vets with Tosco yesterday and I saw your signs there. You must have covered every inch of Maple Falls."

Tosco happened to be a very pampered Pomeranian that Big Red despised and due to his nipping of ankles habit, Maddie wasn't exactly fond of him either but couldn't find it in herself to say a word against him, because she knew Suzy would be devastated that everyone didn't feel the same way about her beloved pet.

When you loved your animal, it was hard to find any fault, which was something she knew firsthand. Pedigree or not.

"I have them in every shop and on every lamppost in town and even some on the outskirts. The reward will be in the Destiny Tribune tomorrow and was in our local paper today. Bernie said next time he has to take a fare or pick someone up from the airport, he'd drop a few of the flyers into some businesses there. Animal rescue are keeping an eye out for him too."

Suzy nodded enthusiastically. "I've had another idea. We've already used the phone tree through the school, but why not tackle the actual phone book?"

"How do you mean?" Laura asked.

"We split it up into sections and, with the help of the school phone tree, we phone everyone in the county. Just to be sure we haven't missed someone."

Maddie felt a renewed surge of hope. "What a fantastic idea. The more people know the better the chance of getting him back."

"Let's do it," Angel agreed.

"I'll organize it. We'll each have a section, plus I'll rope in some volunteers. I'll contact them and give them their portion of the phone book to work from."

"That's a lot of work for you, Suzy."

"I want him back as much as you do. I can't bear to see you so down, and I know how I'd feel if it were Tosco."

As they left, Suzy put her hand on Maddie's arm. "I'll be in touch tomorrow with the names of who's helping us and which section everyone has."

Maddie hugged her. "That's wonderful. I appreciate the trouble."

"It's no trouble. You'd do it for Tosco."

Maddie nodded. Certainly, she'd like to believe she would. A noise made her turn to face the bathroom, where Laura was exiting.

"I thought you had gone with Angel?"

"I wanted to talk to you."

"Sure, but it's dark outside, and you walked here."

Laura waved away her concern, determined to speak. "I'll be fine. I've been thinking about what you said about what good it could do going to the Country Club on Friday."

"Please, don't. I was immediately sorry to have brought it up and for making you feel bad."

"No. You're right. I can help, so I will. It's time to stop letting my past dictate my future."

"Wow, where did that come from?"

"You. Things in your life weren't making you happy so you changed careers. I've made a small inroad by taking a job with you and saying no to my parents in their bid to have me run for Mayor a second time. At twenty-nine, it was high time. I need to continue the trend. That means standing up for myself when I'm being bullied. Every time."

Maddie made a sympathetic noise. "It isn't as easy as it sounds, is it?"

"It isn't, and I appreciate you get that."

"What's the plan then?" Maddie asked.

Laura shrugged. "You tell me."

"I want to get in so I can confront Mickey with other people as witnesses. I don't believe Irene Fitzgibbons will put up much of a fight, so I might speak to her on a one-to-one basis. She has a cat, so I could appeal to her empathy on that score. Do you think you'll get the tickets easy enough?"

"You mean because my parents threatened to disown me? When I picked them up from the airport it was hardly mentioned so I don't think getting tickets will be an issue at all. Despite mother thinking I'm an embarrassment."

"You're being very brave, and I'm proud of you for standing your ground. Although, I may be a little selfish in wanting tickets to an event that could make both of us ill." Maddie grimaced.

"I'm only brave because I have all of you. I feel stronger, and more capable of dealing with them somehow. Plus, I have no intention of throwing away the only job I've got on my own, and more importantly enjoy, despite their threats. I don't want them to have the power to hurt me anymore."

Maddie's heart swelled. "I'm so glad. If you need any of us, you just holler and we'll be there."

Laura grinned. "Thanks. I may need to take you up on that, depending on how long they stay."

When she left, Maddie called Gran. She needed to know that Laura got home safe and Gran understood completely. They chatted until she heard Laura arrive at the cottage.

Now she could go to bed and only worry about Big Red, and a party she had no stomach for.

Chapter Twenty

Maddie had just opened and was stocking the cookie trays when the door chimed. Angel came in wearing a chiffon concoction that flowed about her as she walked.

"Coffee," she demanded from the doorway.

Maddie laughed. "What can be that bad?"

"I have the last of the blue brigade coming in this morning, to get them ready for the party tonight."

Laura came through from the kitchen to make the coffee. "I guess they'll all be going?"

Angel nodded. "For sure. It's their stomping ground, after all. I'm thinking there will be plenty of discussion over Maude's death in the salon today."

"I'd be surprised if there wasn't. How's Beth doing?" Maddie asked.

"She's a marvel. I'm managing much better now. She doesn't mind doing all the cleaning and people are saying her shampooing is better than mine." Angel tried to look outraged, but couldn't hide her pleasure. "I'm hoping some of them will allow her to try her hand at putting in rollers."

"I'm so glad. It seems like our staff issues have been resolved." Maddie turned to find Luke at the doorway staring at Angel. It wasn't an oddity with men folk, but he'd never done it before. "Everything okay?"

"What? Oh, yes." He hurriedly moved back into the kitchen like he'd been caught with his hand in the cookie jar.

Maddie shrugged as she and Angel shared a quizzical look.

"Boys," they said together, then laughed.

"I'd better get back, before they arrive." Angel said.

"Actually, I've been meaning to ask you for a haircut."

"Anytime, you know that."

Maddie nodded. "Tell me when you're free, and only if you let me pay."

"Don't talk crazy. We're best friends. I must owe you a million haircuts for all the baking you throw my way."

"That's different and I don't throw food."

"Don't start that again, detective. We're all offering a service. Therefore, it's a fair exchange."

"Don't let the sheriff hear you call me that."

Angel grinned. "Especially when we have our first real detective in town, who happens to be very good-looking." She winked. "How about super sleuth?"

Maddie's hands went to her hips. "How about none of the above? Are you going to let me pay or not?"

"No, I am not. It's not like you're in my shop every day or even every week. Unlike me coming in here sometimes twice a day."

Maddie groaned. "But you pay."

"That doesn't account for all the extras. On top of that, both you and Gran feed me a couple times a week." Angel gave her a serious look, which did more than all the joking around. "Please. I want to do something for you, but you're always so independent. It would make me feel good."

The lump in Maddie's throat made it difficult to answer for a few seconds. "Darn. You had me at please."

Angel gave a winner's grin. "Phew, I am so glad that's settled. Late afternoon? I should be finished by then and you'll end the workday on a good note."

"I'll be there."

Maddie walked into the kitchen, shaking her head, knowing she'd been played. Luke was wiping down surfaces and Laura frowned.

"I've done all those," she said.

"What? Oh. Yes. I forgot."

Something was clearly bugging him.

"I'm just going to take the rubbish out."

Laura gave Maddie an odd look and when he shut the door behind him, she peeked out the window from behind the curtain.

"Why are you checking up on him?"

Laura didn't turn away. "I'm worried. He already put the rubbish out."

"Perhaps he forgot?"

"I don't think so. He's outside Angel's garden now." Laura had practically bent herself in half, with her head twisted at an odd angle, so she could see up the road. "He's talking to Beth. They look like they're arguing."

Maddie was intrigued. "I didn't know they knew each other. Did you?"

"Not until today. You don't suppose they're an item, do you?"

"I have no idea what to think. Angel might know."

Chapter Twenty-One

As arranged, Maddie went to the salon. Beth greeted her in a very professional manner and waited until she'd undone her braid and shaken it out before showing her to one of Angel's two chairs.

"You have beautiful hair Ms. Flynn." Beth wrapped a plastic cloak around her.

"Thank you. Please call me Maddie."

The girl gave a small smile in the mirror. "You must have been growing it forever.

"Maybe not forever, but I hardly ever cut it because it only gets tied up." It really had been years and her braid was now down to her lower back. "It's darn heavy and takes forever to dry."

"Are you getting much off?"

She turned to her friend at the reception desk working on a computer. "What do you think, Angel?"

Angel tapped a long nail on her lower lip. "I think a few inches is all we need. Why mess with such gorgeous hair that everyone envies?"

Maddie grinned at the compliment. "There you go. My hairdresser has spoken."

Beth smiled as she reclined the chair and Maddie thought how much more attractive she was when she did so. Then she was treated to the most wonderful shampoo.

She hadn't felt this relaxed for some time. If ever. "This is heaven."

Angel walked passed and grinned at her expression.

"Isn't it. I had Beth practice on me a few times before I let her loose on the clients and I knew she had a gift right away. She's a natural."

Beth blushed with pleasure, and Maddie sighed. "I totally agree. I could start coming in every week for this."

Angel laughed and went to answer the phone.

The hands in her hair stilled for a moment, as if Beth forgot she was there.

"Everything okay?"

In the mirror she could see Beth check that Angel had taken the phone out the back of the salon. Her hands began to move again, but not quite as before. Then she leaned down, speaking softly into Maddie's wet ear.

"Those animals that went missing . . ."

Maddie felt a shiver run down her back and it wasn't the water that Beth had inadvertently dripped down there. "Yes?"

"Some got returned, right?'

"They did. Although it was only a couple. My cat is still missing, and I believe there are far more than we know about in the same situation. Why do you ask?"

"I was worried about them. How many do you think there are?"

"I can't say for sure, but I think more than a dozen. Stealing pets is a despicable thing to do, isn't it?"

There was silence for a few moments, and Maddie waited, unsure where this was going, but knowing that this wasn't a random conversation.

Beth rinsed her off, then began a conditioning treatment and resumed the conversation.

"It isn't right. But they might just be lost, isn't that so?"

"If they were lost, some of the owners wouldn't have received ransom letters." Maddie's voice came out a little harsh.

Startled, Beth drew in a deep breath. "Surely, the animals will be looked after?"

"I'm hoping so, but imagine if you were taken from your family without warning? With no way of getting back to them. Big Red is part of my family, just as I'm sure the others are to their owners. The animals and owners are suffering."

"I guess it would be awful."

"Let's just say that carrying on as normal is darn hard when he's constantly on my mind. I had no brothers or sisters so Big Red fills a huge gap."

She could feel the emotions bubbling up as her words caught in her throat, and Beth glanced into the mirror.

"I'm sorry, I didn't mean to upset you."

"That's okay. I'm a bit of a softie when it comes to animals in general, but that big cat of mine is so much more than a pet."

Beth gave a shaky smile and renewed her efforts on Maddie's hair. It really was so good, and she managed to relax, but not quite as much as before. When the teenager had finished, she toweled her off and led her to a chair where Angel was now waiting to do the cutting.

"Angel, do you mind if I take a break?"

"Go ahead, Sugar. The next appointment is in half an hour, so take your time."

Beth went through the small lunchroom and out the back door, shutting it behind her.

Tires squealed in Plum Place and Angel tutted. "That'll be the boyfriend on his bike. He never leaves her alone."

The sound had put Maddie's teeth on edge. "What do you mean?"

"He's always here to drop her off or pick her up, which is fine, but he hangs around each time she has a break as well."

"Isn't that kind of sweet?"

"No, I don't think it is. Not when Beth comes back looking like she's been crying. And other things."

Angel and Maddie didn't have secrets, so her hesitation was odd.

"What other things?"

Angel made a rude noise. "I swear she has a bruise on her cheek. From two days ago."

"Like she'd been hit?"

"Exactly. Beth tries to cover it with make-up, but growing up the way I did I can spot that kind of thing a mile away."

Maddie hadn't seen the boyfriend, but she hated violence and immediately wanted to protect the girl. "That's terrible. What can we do about it?"

"You know, I hadn't decided to do anything, but just saying this aloud makes me think I will say something."

Angel was clearly upset with herself over her lack of action.

"If it's what you think and she wants to press charges, we can get Ethan involved."

"Good idea. It may take a while to get the opportunity. I

don't want her to be upset around customers, or embarrass her by having them overhear her business."

"Let me know how it goes. I hate the thought of anyone touching a woman that way."

"Sugar, there's a lot of it going on. Doesn't make it right, but it doesn't get any easier for women to complain about it."

"Some people have a funny concept of love." Maddie couldn't help thinking of her ex, Dalton, who couldn't understand why she was so upset when she caught him having a fling with her flat mate. Although he never laid a hand on her, he thought they could carry on their relationship as if nothing happened, and even tried to spin it that it was somehow her fault.

"Isn't that the truth."

If anyone could understand it was Angel. Marrying their high school football star had given her nothing but heartache. And plenty of bruises. They gave each other a sympathetic look in the mirror.

"Anyway, you haven't said who this boy is?" Maddie asked.

"He's never come in, so I don't know. Beth doesn't talk about him either. I don't think she even likes the boy, otherwise why does she look so scared every time she leaves with him?"

"I really don't like the sound of that at all. Please talk to her soon, Angel. It would be awful if something happened to her."

Angel shivered. "I'd never forgive myself."

As she walked back to the bakery, Maddie had a vision of Laura watching Luke argue with Beth.

Surely, the boy Beth was seeing couldn't be Luke. Could it?

Chapter Twenty-Two

Ethan stopped by after closing to see how Maddie was doing. He was in the kitchen, with his hat in his hands, eyebrows raised at the leftover box Luke had packed before he left.

"Go ahead. Take as much as you like."

"Aren't these being donated?"

"They get picked up every other day and I don't keep anything with cream just in case it goes bad."

His eyes widened at the selection and after his hand hovered over various items several times, he took a chocolate éclair and a seat at the counter. She almost laughed at the look on his face as he took his first bite. It reminded her how she'd felt earlier today when she'd experienced the shampooing from Beth.

"Have you seen Angel today?"

He had a little cream on the edge of his mouth and as strong as the urge was to wipe it away, she handed him a napkin instead.

He grinned as he took the hint, after cramming the rest

in his mouth. "Angel? Not today. Although I can see you have. Your hair looks gorgeous. Why?"

She waved away his compliment, secretly pleased he'd noticed. They were alone, so Maddie decided to relay their conversation about Beth.

His eyes hardened. "I've noticed she gets scared every time she sees me. Now I know why. She's protecting this guy, whoever he is."

"Please don't say anything to Beth until Angel's had a word. This needs a delicate touch."

"I won't, but if I'm going to be effective, I'll need a name."

Maddie kept the fear to herself about Luke, because she truly couldn't believe it of him. "None of us have seen him. What about the license plate of his bike? We could keep a lookout?"

"That will do nicely. Even if it's not his, it will give us a place to start. You've got a good head for this business."

She took his compliment and ran with it. "What happened to the person who was killed in that car crash near Destiny?"

His hat got a severe twisting. "No, Maddie. You are not getting involved in this any more than you are."

She chewed her top lip for a moment. "So, it did have something to do with the case?"

He threw his hands in the air. "Which case? They could all be separate incidents for all we know."

"Sure, and a roll is the same as a croissant."

"Ahhh. Okay?"

"You know what I mean. There is no such thing as coincidence."

Sighing, he looked longingly at the tray. "What have you been reading up on now?"

She pushed the tray closer to him. "What can I say? I like research."

Ethan shook his head and reluctantly pushed it away. "Well stop it, and stop trying to feed me. It's called 'bribery and corruption'."

"Are you telling me what to do again?" she teased.

His mouth twitched in that cute way he had. "I don't think I can answer that."

"Pleading the fifth amendment are we?"

"If that's what it takes for you not to tangle me up with your twisted logic."

"Logic that is often right."

He raised his eyebrows. "It's not a game. With a murderer, and a kidnapper, albeit only around animals so far, you're safer away from this."

The idea of being kidnapped again made her a little queasy, but she was already involved, and he looked away while he continued.

"I'm very fond of Big Red. I don't know any of the others, but I'm doing the best I can for all of them."

So that was it. He felt he was letting her down. "Your commitment isn't in question. It's just that time is marching by and no one is coming forward. People are keeping secrets that must be uncovered soon, if the animals have any chance. Imagine those owners who love them like I love Big Red. Can you see that it is a terrible place to be? The not knowing?"

He looked pained. "Point taken. Perhaps I don't understand it the way you do, or have the appreciation for pets the way other people do. There are guidelines for how I do my job, but maybe I could try another approach."

Maddie felt a surge of excitement, resisting the urge to do a fist pump. "Yes!"

He grinned, his dimple flashing, and Maddie had to take a step back from all that handsomeness. He was listening, and he would try harder. That had to be enough for now. And, the way he looked at her was too much right now. When they were done with searching for Big Red and the rest, when the murderer was found, maybe then they could find time for themselves.

Just then the sound of squealing tires had Maddie running to the door, she slammed out of it so hard that the handle smashed back against the wall as she jumped down the stairs and ran along the path to the walk.

By the time she got there, the vehicle had disappeared around the corner.

"What the heck, Maddie?" Ethan was beside her, looking at her like she had a screw loose.

"That was the boy's bike. The one Beth gets picked up on each night."

"Are you sure?"

"I hear it every day. Who else drives down Plum Place like that? Teenagers don't bother in case Gran sees them and tells their parents. This driver obviously doesn't know Gran. Or doesn't care."

His mouth dropped open for a second. "Is that her coming this way?"

Someone was coming down the street from the cottage. While it couldn't be said she was running, Gran was certainly moving at a cracking pace, with Laura hot on her heels. Nearly seventy-year-olds, didn't move this way unless something was amiss.

Maddie ran up the street. "Gran, what's happened?" she yelled when they were within shouting distance. Gran thrust something at Laura and pushed her in front, whereby she ran to Maddie, her red bun bobbing furiously.

"You have a note," she said as she stopped in front of Maddie, gasping for breath. "A ransom note. There was no envelope. It was on the rocker, when we heard the squeal of tires, it reminded us of when Mrs. Oliver was run over. We ran outside and found this."

Ethan was a lot quicker than she was. He snatched at the note before Maddie had a chance. She stood on tiptoes looking over his shoulder.

"If you want to keep your monster of a cat alive, be at the quarry at the end of town 7pm tomorrow night. Bring one thousand dollars. You will receive directions to find the cat once the money has been paid. Put the money into the bag you'll find under the left-hand corner of the tank. No police or no cat."

"Thank goodness!" she said, as Gran arrived, out of breath and red cheeked.

"Madeline Flynn!" She waved a finger. "You are not going to any quarry."

"Gran . . . It's Big Red. I have to go."

"Let's take this into the bakery." Ethan said, firmly as he looked around them.

They hurried back down the street and he ushered them inside. Maddie tried to use the time to think of something to make Gran and Ethan see she had to take the risk. They stood at the counter, and, unasked, Laura peeled off to make tea.

"Did either of you see the vehicle clearly?" he asked.

"No, not clearly. We were too late for that, but it was definitely a motorcycle. Black, I think." Laura answered.

Gran was still looking at Maddie with annoyance and fear when Ethan came to her rescue, surprising her as much as the others.

"I have to clear things with the detective, but I'm

thinking that there is no other way to do this, Gran. If Maddie doesn't go, then the petnapper will simply not show." Ethan pulled out all the stops with his soft cajoling voice.

Gran was impervious. She crossed her arms and glared at him. "I won't have Maddie in danger, Ethan. I won't."

He encouraged her to sit, and he took a seat opposite her. "I understand, but I'll be there to watch over her."

"That's all well and good, but can you promise she won't get hurt?"

"You know I can't. But I do promise to do everything in my power to keep that from happening."

"That's not good enough," she said with a stubbornness that only seemed to surface when Maddie was at the heart of things.

Maddie picked up a worn hand. "It'll be all right. If I don't do this and Big Red never comes home, I won't forgive myself and I suspect you wouldn't either."

Gran cradled her hand with both of hers, her lips quivering. "I don't want to lose you again."

Gran had always acted as if she was okay with Maddie's decision to move to New York City. Even when she had stayed to train in a family bakery she had been nothing but supportive. This reminded her again of how unselfish her grandmother was. And, of how loving and caring she had always been.

"I know how you feel, but I can't risk Big Red's life. I'll be careful and do everything Ethan says."

Gran snorted. "That will be the day. I guess you're doing it, no matter what I have to say. Just make sure you don't take any crazy risks."

This was how she had become the Madeline Flynn of today—with a person in your corner who not only protected you fiercely, but also backed you in that same way. It wasn't about giving in; it was to do with not giving up. Gran never had.

Maddie took the still smooth cheeks in her hands and kissed her Gran on both. "You are a marvel," she said sincerely.

Gran held her tight. "And you better not make me regret it."

Over tea they discussed the ransom, which Maddie would collect tomorrow. Luckily the bank had begun opening for a couple of hours on Saturday mornings.

"How did you get on with contacting the other owner's," Laura asked.

Ethan spluttered. "You're doing what?"

"It was easy enough to find the names. Some have never been contacted by the police and I needed to know what the outcome was for each of them."

He sucked in a breath. "And?"

"I just started calling today. Only four would talk to me. They wouldn't say much, apart from their pets were back home and they hadn't had a ransom note."

"That's good, isn't it?" Gran was looking at Ethan for confirmation, but he was watching Maddie.

"I didn't believe them. It was something in their voices that didn't ring true. When I mentioned ransom they got defensive and sounded scared. Plus, six of the numbers are disconnected."

Ethan put his hand over her restless one that had been tapping furiously.

"You've got tonight to get through first. Then the drop tomorrow. I suggest you stop anymore digging until after that otherwise you might scare him or her off."

She slipped her hand out, aware of Gran's keen gaze. "I

agree and I should have thought of that before. My head is in a whirl, but I am ready for tonight. In fact, we should be getting ready, Laura."

Ethan was happy with her capitulation. Her turned to Gran. "I'll be there to keep an eye on her, so don't worry."

"Easy enough to say, but much harder for me to do."

He nodded. "Can I give the two of you a ride home?"

"That would be nice," Gran agreed. Then she hugged Maddie. "Have a little fun if you can and behave yourself."

The sternness was clearly a cover for her fears and Maddie kissed her again, wishing she wasn't so much of a bother, but unable to fix that right now.

Chapter Twenty-Three

L aura and Maddie arrived at the Country Club at seven-thirty. Bernie was having a bumper night with his cab service, but he'd squeezed them into his schedule, and offered to come pick them up if needed. Maddie told him they hoped to get a ride from Suzy who was bringing Angel a little later.

The party was in full swing, with a cacophony of voices rising above the background music from DJ, Noah Jackson.

Maddie wore a blue sheath which had hung in the back of her wardrobe for months. She'd kept her hair down and it hung down her back to her waist. The high shoes, she could have done without. Since she hadn't worn them in so long, her feet were already protesting.

Laura was stunning in a green knee length dress, her red hair sparkled and had also been left down for the occasion. Straightened into submission, it hung around her shoulders.

Several people took second glances.

A waiter offered them champagne, and they took a glass each, since everyone appeared to have one. Someone

Maddie had heard of from Destiny had done the catering, and a waitress wearing a classy apron with 'Jacques' embroidered on the front, hovered with platter of petite tarts and deep fried cheese balls. She politely turned them down, as did Laura. It seemed they were both nervous and Maddie didn't think her stomach could cope with food right now.

"Laura. Come over here, dear."

A tall slim woman with red hair, made a beeline across the room as soon as they entered. She had to be Laura's mother. She was a carbon copy, except her forehead didn't move and her smile did not reach her eyes.

"Mother this is my friend Madeline Flynn. Maddie this is my mother, Eleanor McKenzie."

Maddie extended her hand, which was summarily ignored so she settled for a pleasantry that was instilled in her. "Pleased to meet you." Laura's mother barely glanced at her and looked impatiently at her daughter.

"I'm glad you saw sense about coming tonight. Now that Maude has left us, and Mickey has stepped up to take up her mantle, we'll need everyone to pitch in if we, I mean he, is to win. Let's start you off by circulating with the town committee."

Laura blanched at the imperious look from her mother, but stood a little taller despite it. "I'm not sure how I'll vote until after I hear them both talk."

"You will vote as I say," Eleanor hissed. "After that debacle of an election last time, it's the least you can do."

Laura's eyes glistened, but her shoulders remained square, as she took a sip of her champagne. Maddie sensed that Laura had turned a corner, and no matter how sharp the edges, she would no longer let her mother have an influence on her life. Her father might be a different story.

With clearly more than a few glasses of champagne

under his belt, he was with the group of committee members and other important people, who were standing in the middle of the room. Mr. McKenzie was having a great time telling anecdotes, while Mickey stood beside him, stone-faced.

Laura's mom's attention shifted when she heard her husband's loud guffaw at his own joke. She did not look impressed and marched across the room, forcing a cool smile on her face as she neared them.

It was like watching a train-wreck and Maddie was mesmerized, until Irene Fitzgibbons made her way to them through the crowd, bypassing the group, with a disapproving frown.

"Madeline, I wasn't aware you are a member of our club."

It was more of a statement than a question.

"I'm not."

Irene's nose crinkled as if she had smelled something odious. "The rules are very clear . . ."

"She's my partner for the event," Laura explained.

The nose crinkled further, but after checking that Eleanor McKenzie was standing not so far away, she didn't pursue the matter. "I see. It's a little irregular, but very well."

Maddie couldn't bring herself to say thank you, but she had questions that Irene might know answers to, which was why they were there. Plus, Irene seemed to want to add something as she gave Maddie several furtive glances.

"I'm so sorry about Mrs. Oliver. I know she was a good friend of yours."

"Well, we were friends." Irene took another glance at Laura's mom, and then looked around the room. There was a definite edginess creeping into her demeanor.

"Excuse me, I think the debate is about to begin."

Maddie and Laura shared a look, but said nothing. Meanwhile Eleanor had managed to subdue her husband, and everyone was requested to find a seat. Irene Fitzgibbons and Mickey Findlay took their places on a small stage.

Maddie and Laura found two seats just as the speeches began. Mickey, usually friendly with only those who could help him in some way, seemed to have found some community spirit all of a sudden. He spoke well, making promises that were outlandish and, as intended, they appealed to most of the room.

There were a lot of moneyed people here, some affected by it and some not. Laura, now officially one of the Girlz, seemed more relaxed when she was away from her mom and they spied Angel sitting with Suzy across the room. They had decided to split their resources to increase any chances of overhearing anything useful.

With Mickey droning on, Maddie whispered into Laura's ear. "I want to ask a few questions, but I don't want to scare off the petnapper like Ethan said could happen."

Laura drew in a ragged breath. "Tell me what you want to say."

Maddie grabbed her hand. "Really? Are you sure? I know you hate that sort of thing."

"I'm not sure about much, but if this will help with getting our cat back, then yes, I'm sure."

Loving that Laura thought of Big Red as her cat too, Maddie explained what might work. "But you should say what you think will have the best effect."

"You're putting a lot of faith in me."

"I am, because I know you've got this." With a squeeze of her arm, Maddie moved away from Laura, so that the focus would not be on her.

When Irene spoke after Mickey, there were a few questions directed at both of them. It seemed odd that neither of them mentioned Maude. No one else brought up her name either.

Laura stood, waving at the runner who was taking the hand-held microphone to the those asking questions. They had no way of knowing how much she could say before being shut down. Mickey and Irene frowned as she was handed the microphone. Laura's mother looked wary.

"I'd like to ask our candidates what they propose to do about finding all the missing pets, if elected?" Laura spoke clearly and firmly.

Mickey's smile was cool. His self-confidence at an all-time high. "That's a matter for the Sheriff's department, Ms. McKenzie."

"Do you know if anyone here has a missing pet?"

He shrugged, then laughed. "I don't see how knowing that would help anything."

"It could tell us the exact area the kidnappers are targeting and how wide-spread it is"

"As far as I know most of the animals wandered off. I think we should move on to things to do with Maple Falls," he said dismissively.

"You don't think missing animals, ransom letters, and a murder, has anything to do with Maple Falls?"

"They are completely separate issues. The murder is being investigated, as you well know. Animals go missing all the time. I hardly think it's a matter to concern ourselves with."

That caused a buzz in the room.

Mickey heard it and made a sad face. "Of course, it's a terrible business, and when the murderer is caught resources will, I'm sure, be pushed into that direction."

"One last question, if I may?" Laura didn't wait for his answer and addressed the room loudly. "Is anyone here missing a pet? And, have they received a ransom letter?"

A deafening silence fell over the room. Maddie who was standing at the back, heard a chair scrape near her and a woman left very quickly. Even craning her neck, she couldn't see who it was, before the general hubbub began.

"Since the answer is clearly no, I suggest we move on," Mickey said with more than a touch of animosity. "And perhaps you could pass the word, Ms. McKenzie, that there will be a meeting at the community center for those that aren't a member of the Country Club. I'm sure you have plenty of contacts who fall into that category."

Laura handed back the microphone and sat down.

He could be as condescending as he liked, now that Laura had achieved what Maddie intended, which was to alert everyone here that there were others in the same situation and they should join together to put an end to the petnapping. The rest was up to Ethan.

He'd been standing all this time near the door. They hadn't acknowledged each other, but she saw him slip out after the woman who'd just left. She hoped he would find her and get to ask her some questions, since the ones in the room dried up about then.

Laura came and found her as soon as she could. "Let's go out into the garden."

They squeezed passed several people who gave them curious glances, and she hoped they had been given food for thought. Once they were outside in the small courtyard that opened to the golf course, she hugged Laura.

"Well done. I'm so proud of you. I hope your parents won't give you a hard time over it?"

Laura shook her head. "Don't worry about that. Mom's

got her hands full getting Dad to stop drinking and he's in no condition to argue. They can say what they like tomorrow, but I'm done with all this. I'm more worried over the way Mickey looked at us."

"What do you mean?"

"He's mighty annoyed. He knows how to woo a crowd, but he has a terrible temper and I may have lost him some votes around the issue of the missing pets."

"That's true. You do need to be careful." Irene Fitzgibbons, stepped from behind the statue that had hidden her approach, making both women jump back.

"How do you mean?" Maddie wasn't sure how to take the comment. Was it a threat?

Irene looked about her, fear in her eyes. "Mickey wants to be Mayor, and he's not leaving anything to chance."

"Isn't that why you're running against him."

"He'd like everyone to believe that. The truth is I had no choice." She bit her lip hard and looked around once more. When she continued her voice was barely above a whisper. "My Peanut is missing. It's been four days."

Maddie was blown away. "Peanut? Is that your dog?"

"Not just any dog. He's a pedigree dachshund." Her lips trembled. "When he was smaller, I carried him in a special bag wherever I went."

"I'm very sorry, Mrs. Fitzgibbons, but why are you telling us this?"

"Because I've done everything I was asked to do. Peanut, is still gone."

Maddie's fingers drummed along her thigh. "You have to run for Mayor? Is that part of the deal?"

"Of course it is. I don't want to be Mayor. I like my life just as it is. Or was."

"Then why?"

"If I don't run, the election won't seem legitimate, because he," she nodded vaguely in Mickey's direction, "won't have any competition. All I have to do is pretend I want the job."

"What if everyone votes for you?"

She frowned. "That's my point. As unlikely as it seems, if that happens, I'm scared I will end up like Denise and Maude."

As much as Maddie didn't particularly want to vote for Irene, she absolutely wouldn't vote for Mickey. Would the people of Maple Falls feel the same, even here, at the Country Club, which was surely full of people who might want him to win? The old boy network was alive and well. But then again, Mickey had trodden on a lot of toes recently, and the stink of the last election hung on him, whether he liked it or not.

"Could I take a look at the ransom letter?"

Mrs. Fitzgibbon raised an eyebrow. "It's not with me. I hid it, just in case. I can't go tell the sheriff because the note is not in Mickey's handwriting and you know how clever he is. But you could. You and Sheriff Tanner are very good friends. If you could explain my predicament, I'd appreciate it, but it must be a secret. If the kidnapper hurts my Peanut, I don't know what I'll do," her voice hitched and she glanced around once more. "I must go."

She backed away and walked around the other side of the column as if she hadn't been baring her soul to a person she'd rarely spoken to before today.

Chapter Twenty-Four

Laura and Maddie found Ethan outside the main doors.

"We know who the kidnapper is," Laura blurted.

"Shush." With a finger on his lips he motioned them down the driveway.

They passed a few people who were leaving and Maddie tried not to act differently, but she was just as excited as Laura, who apologized as soon as they were alone.

"Sorry, I wasn't thinking."

"It's okay, Laura. I don't think they heard you. Just remember you can't go around accusing anybody without hard evidence."

"We have it. Irene Fitzgibbon just explained to us why she's running for mayor." Maddie told him the sordid details and was disappointed when he merely nodded.

"So, now you can arrest Mickey, can't you?" Laura asked.

"That's not how it works. Unless we have physical

proof, we can't even suggest he's guilty. He had an alibi for the time of the murder, so if he did orchestrate it, then he has someone doing his dirty work. That's the person I want right now."

She was astounded. "We do nothing?"

"You've both done enough. Leave this to me. If he thinks we're on to him, things could get way more dangerous than they already are."

"Won't he think that anyway, after the things I said to him?"

Ethan hesitated, then sighed. "You're right. Come on, I'm taking you both home."

They followed him to his sedan, but Maddie wasn't done yet. She waited until they were out of the gate before turning to face him from the passenger seat.

"Who was the woman who ran out of the room?"

He sighed. "You can't breathe a word of this. She's Maude's sister. They were very close as children and young women. Apparently, not so much lately. She came to town purely for the funeral on Tuesday. She's struggling with the thought of Maude being murdered and wants to help us, which is why she came tonight, but she's also scared of Mickey."

Maddie sat back. "Mickey wants the mayor's job, far more than we gave him credit for. How many candidates must die before the town simply gives in to him?"

He glanced side-ways and grabbed her busy hand. "Calm down, Maddie. We have leads and we have witnesses. Now we just need to connect the dots so that the trail lands squarely at his door."

He dropped Laura, who has listened quietly from the back seat, at Grans, then took Maddie home, walking her to the door.

"I didn't get a chance to say how lovely you look in that blue dress. It matches your eyes perfectly."

"Please don't Ethan. I know you're trying to take my mind off things, but it's not going to work tonight."

He pushed one long strand of hair over her shoulder. "Fair enough. I'm doing my best, you know?"

There was pain in his voice, and it made her sad. "I do know. You're a great sheriff, and maybe I don't tell you that enough, but like it or not, Big Red is still missing."

"I get how much he means to you, and I'm sorry it's taking so long."

She nodded. "It's not your fault."

Smiling, he took her key and opened the door. Pushing her gently inside he kissed her forehead. "Tomorrow's going to be rough, so try to get a good night's sleep and make sure you lock up properly."

He waited until she'd done so before he left and suddenly she wished that he'd stayed.

Maddie knew she wasn't girlfriend material in this state, but her patience was wearing thin. She didn't want people scared, hurt, or killed. She just wanted Big Red, safe at home, where he belonged.

It didn't seem too much to ask.

Chapter Twenty-Five

When Maddie took the catering job for a birthday party today, she hadn't counted on delivering a ransom.

Tonight, if she did as she was asked, she would have Big Red back. She and Laura worked without discussing it, but there had been shared looks and their worry was palpable.

Gran had been there first thing in the morning, but Maddie had been unable to keep both of them calm and asked her to go home so that Luke didn't find out what they were up to. She would have liked him to go as well, but the baking wouldn't do itself.

For this first time ever, Maddie's hands shook as she baked. Nothing she did made it any better, so she decided to step away from the kitchen until she had the money organized for the ransom.

"Laura, I'm heading over to the bank before it closes."

Her friend gave her an understanding look, but said nothing. Luke was in the shop using the counter space to pack up the order since the bakery wasn't open to the public.

She collected her bag and made the short walk across Maple Lane and through a walkway. There were the usual amount of people around for a Saturday, with some taking advantage of the new opening hours to do their banking.

Claire, a recent addition to the staff was behind the counter and smiled when Maddie stepped up to it.

"Going on a shopping trip?" Claire asked, carefully counting the money.

"I'm not sure."

The woman placed the money into an envelope and passed it under the grill. "I didn't mean to pry."

"That's okay." Maddie stowed it inside the largest handbag she owned. "I have a few things to get, so we'll see how far the money goes. You know how it is."

Claire grinned. "I do. Never far enough in my book."

Maddie left quickly, before there were more questions. She was in such a hurry that she bounced into Ethan's broad chest as she came out onto the sidewalk.

His hands grabbed her upper arms, making sure she didn't fall. "Where's the fire?"

"No fire."

"Are you okay? You look like you've seen a ghost."

"No ghost." She pushed passed him, but he followed her out into the sunshine.

Maddie figured he would go, since she obviously wasn't encouraging the conversation, but as she headed back to the shop, he kept pace beside her. She stopped and turned, hands on hips. "Can I help you with something?"

Ethan gave her an appraising look. "I'm all good. I suspect you aren't, so I'm walking you home."

"Don't be silly. I'm fine."

"When you say fine, I know you mean anything but fine."

He knew her too well. She shrugged. "It's hard to pick one emotion at this point."

"I get it."

His words were gruff, yet she could see he was making sure she was okay. It seemed they both had a lot riding on tonight's outcome.

When she got to her shop, she hesitated. "I have fresh scones, if you'd like one?"

"How is that even a question? Let's go."

She couldn't help a tight smile. Ethan soothed her jitters. It was going to be a long day, and a distraction in the form of the handsome sheriff wouldn't hurt at all.

Laura was in the shop with Luke, checking the order. She gave them a smile of relief when she saw they were together. Perhaps she thought Maddie might get robbed, which had crossed her own mind. This business was affecting them all.

"Ethan's staying for a bit, then I'll close. Are you okay to drop off the order?"

"Of course. Luke said he'd drive me," Laura said with a telling look.

"Thanks, both of you. And, for all the work you've done this morning."

Luke gave her an awkward smile and took out the last boxes to his car.

Maddie walked Laura to the door.

"I told him you need a car, so I've left my car keys on the counter, and it's parked outside." Laura suddenly embraced her, whispering in her ear, "Stay safe, Maddie." Then she bolted down the path, a hand to her mouth.

Maddie took a moment to compose herself, before returning to face Ethan. "Coffee?"

"Please."

She bustled about, placing a plate and knife in front of him and set a place for herself. He sat watching her and she felt a little self-conscious as she handed him his coffee. "I'm just going to warm the scone for a few seconds since they were made early this morning."

"Will it come with melted butter?"

She forced a grin. "You sound like Angel."

That made him laugh. "Soon she'll be baking her own. You know, I had considered joining your class, if you get another one going."

"You?"

He waggled an eyebrow. "I hope that's not a sexist remark, Ms. Flynn?"

She shook her head. "The thing is, I don't know if my ladies would be able to concentrate with a man like you around."

His cheeks turned slightly pink. "I'm not sure whether to be flattered or insulted. Perhaps my role as sheriff could make them feel intimidated."

Intimidated wasn't the word she was thinking of. "I hadn't considered that. Good point."

He smiled wryly. "It's a shame though. It would have been one way to spend more time with you."

Maddie collected the scone and placed a butter dish in front of him along with his coffee. He was still waiting on an answer and she couldn't respond with the one he wanted. "Ethan," was all she said by way of a warning. One he wasn't about to heed.

He slathered his scone in butter and took a healthy bite, clearly his appetite wasn't compromised.

She poured herself tea but elected to stand. "Something's wrong with Luke."

He shut his eyes, as if she were driving him crazy. *Nothing new there*, she thought.

"Tell me."

She grimaced. "He apparently knows Beth."

"It's a small town."

"They were arguing."

He carefully put down his cup. "You think he's the one hurting her?"

"I don't. But I get the feeling he knows something."

"And you didn't ask him? That's a first. There's no time to do that now." He frowned. "So, you picked up the money?"

She nodded, knowing he knew why she had been at the bank, and suspecting that Ethan had been keeping track of her for some time. "It's in that bag."

She'd put in on a shelf by the walk in and they both stared at it like it was the cause of their worries.

"You should probably put it somewhere safe."

"I can't imagine anywhere safer than in a room with the sheriff."

He laughed.

"Although, it did say no police. What if someone saw you come in here?"

"They always say that, and I'm in here most days, getting food."

"I know. It's just that it reminds me of all those letters when poor Denise was murdered and you're not usually here on a Saturday."

"Let's talk about tonight." He pushed his plate away. "Are you prepared?"

"As ready as I'll ever be. Laura's kindly lending me her car, so I hope that I can keep that safe too."

He nodded. "It will be fine. I'll get the license plate and

193

details to make it easy to follow you from a distance. You won't see me, so don't panic. I'll be close by. You do the drop and come straight home. Here. Not Gran's."

"I get it. I don't want Gran or Laura hurt."

"It's just a precaution. As soon as you leave, I'll follow the car that picks up the money."

"It sounds dangerous."

"A lot less dangerous than you doing all this by yourself. Besides, I've done stuff like this before, and I'll have my deputies stationed around in unmarked cars."

"What about the detective?"

He raised an eyebrow. "Don't you worry about him. He's got his job to do and I am not discussing it with you, so don't ask."

Ethan sounded adamant.

"I'm glad you have backup, but what if they see you? Big Red might be killed and I.. ."

He leaned across the table and took her hands. "This is the best way I can think of to do it, so get your pretty head around it, because I'm not letting you meet a kidnapper, or potential killer, alone. This way, we all have back-up. Okay?"

Her hands tingled in his and Maddie knew this battle was lost. Maybe it wasn't the only one. With the way they argued she wasn't sure how a relationship between them might ever be possible, but she was drawn to the idea of it. More so with every day that passed.

Ethan made her feel safe even when the world appeared hell bent on destroying her peaceful existence.

Chapter Twenty-Six

Maddie drove slowly up the rickety driveway to the rusted silo with Ethan's instructions running through her head. Once he left her, it turned into an incredibly long afternoon.

The petnapper was probably out there somewhere, which was scary, but knowing that Ethan was watching out for her helped to keep her calm enough to go through with the plan.

She pulled into a large gravel area, sweeping in a large arc so that she parked facing back the way she'd come. Night had begun to fall, and a beautiful sunset made the sky glow. Unfortunately, the color of blood sprang to mind, thus destroying any pleasantness.

Checking her mirrors and seeing no one about, she slowly opened the door and listened. Apart from the sound of crickets, the country was eerily silent. She got out, hefting the plastic shopping bag she'd put the money in, and walked to the bottom of the silo where she'd been instructed to put it.

A brown bag lay there, partially hidden by dried grass.

Made of very old leather, it was an effort to force the money inside and zip it closed. She pushed it back to where it had been and walked warily back to Laura's car. Sensing eyes on her, Maddie's skin prickled with unease.

She couldn't wait to get away, and as soon as she got inside the car she locked the doors. Her foot hit the gas a little heavily and the tires kicked up stones producing a slight skid on her way out of the parking area. Her eyes darted left and right but all she could see was scrub and trees.

A vision of the petnapper jumping from his hiding place had her heart pounding, but she made it to the end of the gravel road without him doing so and pulled onto the road proper.

"Please catch him, Ethan. Please save Big Red," she said aloud, her voice strangled by tears. Adrenaline was all very fine until you'd finished with it.

As soon she got home, she called Ethan. "I'm back."

"You did good. I'm proud of you. He has it. Let's keep the line clear. I'll call you when I have news."

"Okay." Maddie felt warmth at his praise seeping into her, but it wasn't enough to make her forget the danger he was in. She could tell by the sounds in the background that he was driving; hopefully still tailing whoever had picked up the money. "Ethan?"

"Mmmm?"

He was probably ten steps ahead of this conversation, but Maddie had to say something. "Be careful. Please."

There was a lengthy silence, and she thought he had gone.

"You sound like you really care," he said softly.

Amid all this drama, she hadn't been expecting that. "Don't be silly, of course I care about my friends."

"Right." He hung up.

Then it occurred to her—what if something happened and she hadn't told him how she felt. Wait. How did she feel? She certainly cared, but knew it was more than that.

During what seemed like hours while she waited, Ethan had managed to give her something else to occupy her mind. Had he done it on purpose? It was a welcome change, but her anxiety was still through the roof. Thinking about what could be happening out there in Maple Falls, to Big Red and/or Ethan, had her pacing the kitchen over and over.

She couldn't resist peeking through her curtains now and again in between cleaning every surface. In the end she did the only thing that might calm her. She baked.

Cupcakes. She could practically make them in her sleep, and when they were done, frosting them could help to keep her distracted. Ethan could take them to Layla's for the boys. After he got back safe. Now she had a reason to begin and found out it was hard to bake with crossed fingers.

She was so engrossed in pouring cake batter into the tins that she jumped when there was a knock at the back door. When she looked through the window, she saw it was Ethan. Dark outside now, she was thankful she had left on the garden lights.

Having locked up tighter than Fort Knox, it took her a minute to unlock everything and remove the chain that Ethan had insisted she get after a break-in she'd had when she first moved in.

"Tell me you have him."

"I'm sorry Maddie. I swapped tailing with a deputy, so he'd be less likely to know he was being followed. Unfortunately, the deputy got a flat tire."

"You're kidding me? After all that, we have nothing." She slumped into a chair.

"I got a license plate. That should help." Even Ethan sounded deflated.

Just then there was a knock on the door. While Maddie opened it, Ethan stood to one side, his hand on his holster. The precaution wasn't necessary. Beth was outside looking agitated.

"I'm sorry to come by so late, Maddie. Can I come in?"

She wanted to say no, but the girl looked frightened and kept looking behind her. Then there was her potential link to the person dropping off that letter. "Of course."

The young woman had only just entered when she saw Ethan. "You have a visitor. I'll come back later."

"No, it's okay I was just leaving. I'll be in touch soon. Don't forget to lock-up." He gave Maddie a knowing look as he went out.

He could have stayed and interrogated Beth, or taken her to the station, but she was here voluntarily and gently might be the best approach. Maddie offered her a seat at the counter and they sat looking at one another.

"What did you want to talk to me about," she prompted.

"Big Red."

Icy fingers gripped her heart. She'd been hopeful, but now she was scared. "Do you know where he is?"

"Kind of, and I know who took him. He took all the animals that have gone missing," her words came out in a rush, interlaced with tears.

Maddie steeled her heart a little. "How would you know that?"

Beth studied the floor, her hands clasped in front of her. "He's kind of my boyfriend."

"Oh, Beth. Not the guy who hurts you? Not Luke?"

"What? You know about that? Gosh no, Luke wouldn't

hurt a fly. He's been looking out for me, trying to find a way to keep me safe."

"Keep you safe from who?" Maddie had to know.

Beth looked down, picked at a hangnail, then gulped back her tears. "It's Johnny, Luke's brother. I feel so bad I didn't say anything, but he threatened me and said he would kill all the animals."

"Are the animals okay?"

"Right now they are, but he's so mad that not everyone is paying what he wants, I don't know what he'll do next. And, they don't have enough food. I promise that I didn't have anything to do with taking them," she ended with a wail.

"Let me call Ethan back."

All color drained from her face, but she nodded, and Maddie went to the alcove to call him.

"She knows," was all Maddie offered, before he admitted to being down the road.

She gathered a box of tissues and came and sat down beside the girl, wanting to drag the information out of Beth, that would lead her to Big Red, but seeing how scared she was, Maddie was worried she might run off.

"How did this start?" she asked, while they waited.

"Johnny said that I had to get a job with you, to find out how close the police were to working out who was taking the animals. I was so relieved when you didn't hire me. I didn't want to be involved, but I ran away from home the week before and he let me stay in a shed his family owns. There weren't so many animals at first and I didn't know they were stolen or about his ransom letters. They were company for me at night. When I realized, I didn't know what to do."

"What changed your mind about telling me? You must know that he'll go to jail?"

"I hope he does. When he brought Big Red and a few more in one day I knew he was stealing them. Then he ran over Mrs. Oliver, even though she wasn't nice to me, that was too much. He said it was an accident, and he was in a state about it, but I don't believe in hurting people or animals. If he hadn't taken her dog, and made her pay more than once, she wouldn't have been trying to catch him."

"Why didn't you say something?"

"Because he wouldn't leave me alone. It was like he was watching me every minute of the day and night. I'm terrified of him, but I couldn't bear it if any animals or someone else got killed. The only way I'll be safe is if he goes to jail."

Maddie was flooded with relief. "You're very brave, and I thank you from the bottom of my heart."

Beth gave her a genuine smile. "I've been the one to feed them because Johnny's scared of the dogs. And Big Red. I took him treats in my pocket so that Johnny wouldn't notice."

"That's my boy." Maddie grinned. "Big Red will be your friend for life."

Ethan didn't knock, and he was gentle with Beth. He waited until Maddie told him what she knew first. Then turned to the scared teenager.

"You've done the right thing, Beth. Now, where can we find them?"

Beth bit her lip for a moment. "I can't tell you, because it's not really on a road, but I can show you. The only thing is he's going to be mighty suspicious when I'm not there since he dropped me off earlier."

"How did you get back to town?"

She picked that nail again. "I walked, then hitched.

Bernie was coming back from dropping someone at the cabins down by the lake. Johnny will do more than hurt me if he finds out I've snitched."

"It's okay. You won't be going," he assured her. "Maddie, do you have a map?"

She nodded. There was a stand in the shop for brochures of the town, along with things to do in Maple Falls. In the back of them was a map of the surrounding area and the walks people could do. She flipped one open and handed it to Beth, who was able to pinpoint the place for them.

Ethan walked to the door and held it open. "I'm dropping you two up to Gran's first."

Maddie picked up her keys. "We can certainly drop Beth off there, but I'm coming with you."

"No, Maddie."

"Yes. If I have to drive Laura's car there myself, I'll do it."

Ethan glared for a moment, then the fight when out of him. "We're wasting time. Let's go."

Chapter Twenty-Seven

"You don't think this is trap. Do you?" Maddie asked as she pointed out an overgrown driveway. Ethan turned and drove slowly along it. "You can never tell, but I've called for back-up to this location."

Without being able to see the back-up that didn't instill too much confidence, but she could see he was concentrating so she let it go.

He hadn't been at all happy about her coming, and nor had Gran or Laura. It had been a tense few minutes, but in the end the time factor had played an important part in settling the matter.

Beth was taken in by Gran and suffered awkward hugs before being inundated with offers of food and drink. The misguided teenager would be well looked after.

Maddie hoped they would be in time to save the animals. Now that Johnny had his money, he might decide to do away with them. She fidgeted in her seat, willing Ethan to drive faster, knowing he couldn't with the path so rutted they were likely to break an axle.

About quarter of a mile later they arrived in a small clearing. At the other end was a wooden building. It loomed out of the night like something from a scary movie. If it was a trap and someone was inside, whoever it was would have heard them arrive and have the perfect vantage point to see them approach.

They both got out of the car. Ethan left his door open and she did the same, unsure if it was for a quick getaway or protection against gunfire. She might have watched too many movies. Her nerves jangled as she waited for whatever came next. Ethan went around the back and came up behind her.

"You stay here. I'll go check it's okay."

"No way."

"Maddie, please," he pleaded. "Do this for me?"

Maddie was shaken by his words and reluctantly nodded. If they were in danger at least she could call the back-up and tell them to hurry. She could see the relief on his face as he crept forward, his hand on the gun that lay in its unclipped holster.

The shed was covered in vines, except for the door which, she could see from here, was slightly warped and had rusty hinges. Ethan stood to one side of the only front facing window and peered through it. He crouched low and did the same when he got to the other side. Then he knocked on the door.

"This is the sheriff. Come out with your hands up."

No one opened the door, but an almighty racket began. Dogs barked, cats meowed, and she thought she could hear birds squawking. Ethan tried the door, and unable to stay back Maddie ran to him. He glared at her, but the noise was so loud here he didn't bother to argue.

He pushed at the door again. It squeaked but didn't

open. Then she heard a sound she recognized—Big Red. No other animal made that sound. His meow was more of a human command. Usually for food, but she just knew he was calling out now for her to set him free.

"Ethan, can you kick this door in? Big Red is definitely in there."

He shook his head. "I'm not a movie star."

Maddie raised her eyebrows. "Really? That's not how the women of Maple Falls feel about you."

"Your faith in me is somewhat misguided, but I can give it a crack," he said, with a small smile.

She moved away and he took a short run-up, then threw his shoulder at the dilapidated door. Crack! Maddie hoped that it was just the door that was badly affected because Ethan emitted a groan as he bounced off it. Then he grinned. The door hung from its hinges, and with a firm shove he managed to push it inwards.

"I knew you could do it." Maddie all but climbed over his back to get inside.

The sound increased ten-fold, and it was clear why. Rows of cats and dogs in cages, at least thirty, were pawing and scraping at their bars. And, there was Big Red right in the middle of them, howling up a storm and looking the worse for wear. He was thinner and had lost some of his fur.

He called out to her, and she opened the cage, pulling him to her chest. He stunk, and she didn't care.

"My poor boy. Are you okay?"

A shadow in the doorway made her turn.

"He's just fine. You, on the other hand, are not."

Johnny stood behind Ethan, an arm around his throat, a gun pointing at her.

"Sorry, Maddie. Have you met Luke's brother?"

She could see that Ethan was furious with himself, and

although she was scared, anger at the man who had stolen these animals and not looked after them properly was the stronger emotion.

"I have, unfortunately," she said through gritted teeth. "You may want to rethink killing a sheriff."

"Maybe, but a cook isn't such a big deal. I might simply injure our friend here and send your monster animal to the big cattery in the sky."

"Don't you dare!"

He laughed. "Or what? You'll hit me with a bagel?"

It was odd that he would bring this up, because she could see bagels on a small table. Were they from her bakery? He was still laughing at her, but neither of these things were as important as keeping Ethan and the pets safe.

"These animals have done nothing to you."

"Really? They're smelly, noisy, and eat too much."

His sneer was like throwing oil on a fire.

"You'd be smelly if you were locked up in a cage, which you will be when our back-up gets here." While she talked, Maddie took note of what weapons were available to her. There weren't too many choices. How could they possibly get out of this mess without them?

"Does she ever shut up?" Johnny asked Ethan. "Seriously, you could do a lot better than this mouthy cook."

Ethan was sending her signals to keep quiet, but she was running on adrenaline again and her mouth wouldn't comply.

"I'm a baker, not a cook. Then again, I wouldn't expect you to know the difference."

In a lightening move Johnny whacked Ethan around the back of his head and he slumped to the floor.

Maddie screamed, while Johnny leapt across the prone figure and slapped her, sending her flying. Big Red, jumped from her arms and up onto the top cage while she landed against the bars of the one he had been in previously. Her ribs protested.

That was when something poked into her. Her back was to Johnny, and she slipped a hand behind her to feel her phone.

"What are you doing? Get away from those animals."

"You pushed me there," she said belligerently, as she turned. Her face throbbed and she could see blood on Ethan's face as he lay on the floor.

"He better be all right—or else." Maddie wasn't sure just yet what she might do, but she would think of something appropriate.

As Johnny came even closer, she flinched. In that moment, perhaps thinking like she did that the man was about to hurt her again, Big Red launched himself from the tier of cages and landed on the criminal's shoulder. He ran his claws down the young man's face, hissing and meowing loudly.

Johnny picked him up and threw him roughly on top of Ethan, then wiped the blood off his cheeks with the back of his hand.

"He's been more trouble than he's worth. You know, no one wants a cat like that. The thing's feral."

Maddie was proud of her boy. "Big Red knows you're not a nice person and he acted accordingly."

"He was lucky that I didn't have the time, otherwise his days would have been numbered a week ago."

Now she felt sick. Thank goodness they'd found him. Found all of them. Except now they were all in danger together."

Suddenly, Johnny looked very young. "Why couldn't you have paid the ransom, and left it, like the rest?"

"The rest?" If he was talking, he wasn't killing, and that had to be a good thing.

"I should have said, 'some' of them. They were only too happy to hand over their cash. It was easy money, until that grumpy Maude Oliver decided to play detective like you."

"I don't understand why you still have all the animals if some already paid you?"

"In the beginning I did give them back. Then I had the idea that if they'll pay once, why not twice?" he scoffed.

Maddie didn't like the glint in his eyes. He looked to be in his early-twenties—not much younger than herself. What had led him down this path? Then she remembered Mickey, and the way he had looked at her.

"Sounds like greed to me. Are you planning on giving any of them back?"

"I wasn't sure until now," he taunted. "With you and the Sheriff interfering it won't be long before others begin to cave, and start blabbing, so you can blame yourself if they don't get their animals. Anyway, since it's getting too hot around here, you'll need to take a drive with me to another location."

Maddie froze. "So you can kill us?"

He sniggered. "I could do that right here if I wanted to."

That didn't make her feel any better. "I guess you have a better way of disposing of us than leaving our bodies in a shed that someone might come by at any time."

"I'm assuming you didn't find this place by accident, so once I've taken care of the snitch, I can come back and empty this place out. Now, get over here, stop causing trouble, and wasting my time."

"All I wanted was my cat back. You're the murderer and catnapper." She didn't want to rile him up, but when she thought of him treating all the poor animals so bad, or killing them, as well as the death of Maude Oliver, and now Ethan, she saw red.

He snarled at her. "You interfered. The last thing I wanted was to take your beast of a cat anywhere. Look at me." He touched his face gingerly. "I've got scratches all over me thanks to that fur ball. Like I said, he's lucky to have survived this long. As for the old lady, that was an accident, not that anyone's going to believe me."

He did look sorry about that, which didn't fit with what he'd just said about killing the animals. Naturally, Maddie was curious, and also desperate to buy some time. For what she wasn't sure of, but she wasn't giving up yet.

Ethan was still prone on the floor, but Big Red, who landed on his feet after attacking Johnny and ran into a corner, was slowly climbing up the cages as if he was stalking the man and getting ready to pounce again. She didn't want that because he might not get away with it after last time.

The animals, apart from two whimpering puppies, were less vocal as they watched Big Red's progress. Maddie wanted his focus anywhere but on Big Red or Ethan.

"Tell me what happened. I'll believe you."

"Sure you will."

His voice was laden with sarcasm. Still, he looked undecided, so she waited quietly, which was no small feat. After a heavy sigh, the words began to pour out and he started pacing.

"She turned up at the park across the road from the bakery as planned. It was already dark when she dropped the money inside the rubbish bin. She waited so long I didn't think she would ever leave. Then she walked away up Maple Lane. I had been hiding in the shrubs at the far edge of the park, so I didn't see where she left her car."

Maddie nodded. "She'd parked down Plum Place, under a tree."

"Which somehow I didn't see, and that's when everything went wrong. My bike was down the end of the street, but it wouldn't start. I tipped it over the hedge, planning to pick it up after the ransoms were all paid, and ran back to get your car. I'd noticed it earlier because you'd left the garage door open." He grinned at her stupidity.

Maddie shuddered at the idea Honey was used as a murder weapon, but it didn't all fit yet. "You would have been coming from the wrong direction to hit Maude."

"You're smart. I'd left the keys for the shed in the lift-up on the bike. I drove down the street with no lights on, got the keys, did a U-turn, and put my foot down. That was when she jumped into the middle of the road. I saw her face only when I hit her. I tried to brake, but I was going too fast and I hadn't seen her with enough time to swerve."

"Where is she? I mean, Honey."

"She? Honey?" he sneered. "No need to worry about that old thing. Now he frowned. "I bet you've been stalling me deliberately. Now you know everything and we really do have to go."

"And if I refuse to go with you?"

Johnny cocked his trigger.

"I'm ready when you are," she capitulated.

He reached into his pocket, throwing something at her as he backed up to the doorway. "Put that plastic tie around the Sheriff's wrists. That's right. Now slip one around yours."

She did as he asked with Ethan, but made a fuss with putting her hands behind her back and trying to tie them.

Frustrated, he yelled, "For goodness' sake, just put it on around the front and use your teeth."

Quickly she did this, hiding her satisfaction.

He checked Ethan's ties, then fished around in his pockets until he found the car keys. After pushing Ethan out of his way with the toe of his boot, he came to tighten hers.

They were cramped in this end of the small shed and Maddie couldn't see a way past the gun. Not that she would leave Ethan and Big Red, even if she could get away. The animals had kept up their noise, and a terrier snapped at Johnny through the bars when he got close.

He smacked the cage making the terrier whimper and cower back as far away as it could. Then he motioned to the door with the gun. "Outside and walk straight ahead. These darn animals are making my head hurt."

Maddie led them back to the clearing where Ethan's blue ford sedan was parked. Johnny opened the doors and she got awkwardly into the back.

"Stay here, if you want the Sheriff to make it."

He went back to drag Ethan, who was probably half as heavy again as Johnny, none too gently to the car. She thought of all the ways she could escape but wasn't prepared to risk Ethan's life.

She moved awkwardly across to give him room, noticing Johnny was sweating by the time he manhandled his prisoner onto the back seat beside her. Ethan was still out cold, and Maddie hoped that it wasn't a serious injury.

Big Red sat by the edge of the path watching them. She hoped he had enough sense to get away from here and sent a silent plea for him to find his way home to Gran if she didn't make it.

Johnny got in the front, dropped his gun on the passenger seat, slammed the door and sped off down the path they'd come up, heedless of the potholes which made it hard for Maddie to keep her seat. Ethan was thrown about like a rag-doll, but luckily he didn't fall off the back seat either.

Instead of heading out to the road he swerved near the top onto an even rougher path. Driving for several miles cross country, they bounced around in the back until he came to a smaller dirt track that went down to the river.

She remembered this place from a walk she'd done as a teenager. It had culminated in jumping off the banks into the chilly lake, then building a fire to dry themselves and toast marshmallows for s'mores.

No one she knew came here anymore because there had been a few slips over the years, making the bank unsafe. This was looking worse by the minute. A vision of the car bobbing at the bottom of the bank, then sinking, came to mind and she clenched her teeth.

Sitting behind the driver's seat, Johnny couldn't see her awkwardly pull her phone from a front pocket. Thankful for staying with her tiny old model and wearing a baggy sweater which had hidden its shape, she had also put it on silent and dimmed the light. At least she hoped she had, as she slowly tapped in 911 before holding it between her thighs.

"Where are you taking us?" she said, loudly.

He glanced in the rear vision mirror. "You'll soon see, now be quiet."

"I know this part of the river. Are you planning on killing the sheriff and me and dumping our bodies at Sam's wharf?"

"Shut up!"

He swerved as a large rut appeared in front and Maddie's elbow whacked against the door, dislodging the phone. She managed to save it from falling, so one more bruise added to the others wasn't so bad.

She wasn't sure if anyone was listening, but she had to give them the best chance of finding them. The only way she could do that was by talking, even though she knew she was making him furious. "Don't do this, Johnny. I can still pay you the ransom."

"Are you kidding me? It's too late for that, now you've seen my face, and I've told you everything." He slapped the steering wheel as they bounced along. "Why the heck did I do that?"

"Because you don't want to do these things anymore. It's a cry for help."

He laughed, in not a particularly pleasant way. "You've been reading too many detective novels. Believe me, I don't want to go to jail, but you'll spill all the details as soon as your boyfriend asks."

"I wouldn't say anything." She crossed her fingers at the lie.

"Really?" He scoffed. "Seems to me that you can't keep your nose out of anyone's business. I kept a low profile around town, but I can see it was a mistake to have Beth around. I bet she told you everything, didn't she? No matter, that little snitch is going to be very sorry."

Scared at her and Ethan's chances of making it out of this situation alive, her determination kicked up a notch. She had more than Big Red and his fellow prisoners to save. Poor Beth was certain to be on Johnny's list of those expendable.

"Did you forget? You came into the shop with your father, didn't you? When you were threatening your brother in front of the sheriff?"

He started cussing about having been forced to go that

day, but Maddie stopped listening to him. She could hear a tapping. It came from beside her and was more of a vibration. Ethan. She almost called out, but pressed her lips together instead. He must have regained consciousness. She couldn't see his face as his head was turned away from her, but it gave her hope.

Luckily, she hadn't been idle. She'd deliberately stretched her palm out when she'd put on the ties and placed her thumbs in between. When he tightened the plastic binding in the badly lit shed, she had only to move her thumbs afterwards to produce a small amount of wriggle room. Slowly, she had slipped her hand from the tie, inch by painful inch before she retrieved her phone.

Watching the rear-view mirror to ensure she wasn't seen, and leaning forward, she plucked the army knife from between her sweaty breasts, then dropped her hands back into the same pose. The first thing she needed after this was a nice bath and a long soak.

She knew it was still the adrenaline that was taking her thoughts to weird places, something she did whenever a crisis reared its ugly head. This certainly qualified and she was grateful for the courage it gave her.

Carefully she reached out to Ethan's back and poked him gently, keeping her hands together, just in case Johnny happened to look back. Swiveling his head, pain evident in his dilated pupils, Ethan frowned, until she showed him the knife. She carefully pressed it into his hands, knowing to try to free him herself would draw Johnny's attention and her plan required two of them to implement.

Ethan slowly and with difficulty cut through the plastic tie on his wrists with difficulty. Finally, they fell away and he looked back at her with relief, one hand clutching the knife.

"Ready?" she mouthed.

He nodded, wincing at the pain, then winked at her. She was so relieved, she forgot for a moment what she was doing, but a glimpse of the lake ahead galvanized her into action. She threw herself forward and wrapped both arms around Johnny's face, effectively blinding him. Her fingers locked around her wrists, and she held on for all she was worth.

"Get the gun!" she yelled. "It's on the front seat."

Chapter Twenty-Eight

E than, already in the process of launching himself over the passenger seat, grabbed the revolver before Johnny could stop him, busy as he was trying to pry Maddie's arms loose.

Hours of kneading dough had made her forearms and fingers incredibly strong, but the punching and twisting were wearing her down, so when Ethan returned the earlier favor by tapping Johnny on the side of his head, not too lightly with the gun, she was more than grateful to have his hands slip from hers.

Until he slumped over the steering wheel, his foot jammed against the accelerator. Now they were rudderless and going faster than ever.

With Johnny's head out of the way, Maddie had a clear view through the windshield. The lake looming ahead wasn't the kind of sight that filled a person with confidence and she couldn't stop a scream when the car plunged off the track and into the long grass of a field, only fractionally slowing them. They bumped headlong down the hill towards a giant oak which was the only thing standing between them and the lake beyond.

From memory, Maddie knew there was a drop behind that tree. A large one. Her stomach lurched along with the car. The momentum taking them on their current trajectory picked up with the increase in the slope.

"I think we should jump!" Ethan yelled.

Maddie yelled back, "We're going too fast."

She was a good driver. Careful and law abiding. Thanks to her grandad wanting her to be safe no matter the situation, she'd learned a thing or two about off-road driving on her summer breaks around places like this.

Not that she had ever been in a situation like this. All she knew was that they had to stop the car to survive. She heaved herself over the front seat, thankful she was still flexible enough, and with one hand pulling hard on the wheel, flinching as Johnny's head bounced a couple of times, her other hand wrenched the hand break. The car bucked and for a moment she thought they would roll. Instead, they skidded sideways a few feet, then smacked headlong into the oak tree.

She could feel herself flying towards the windshield with no way of stopping herself, since her hands had automatically reached up to cover her face. In that last second prior to impact, Ethan grabbed her hips, and yanked her backwards. She bounced onto his lap before they smashed heavily into the front seats, while the car did its best to wrap itself around the tree.

All was quiet except for the hiss from the engine and a few groans from the distressed metal. Untangling their limbs, they stared at each other for a moment or two.

Ethan appeared to be just as surprised as she was to be alive. He touched her face in wonder, and she did the same to him. They both winced at the pain of matching bruising to their foreheads, then grinned like fools. That was when Johnny decided to stir.

Together they peered over the seat. Lucky for him, the kidnapper had remembered to put his seatbelt on. The airbag had all but enveloped him. Even his face was buried in it as he regained consciousness.

Maddie slid off Ethan's lap, so he could get out of the car. He went to the driver's door, yanked it open, and motioned with the gun. "Get out."

Maddie followed and saw the man touch the side of his head tentatively where Ethan had hit him. His eyes cleared. Then he glared at them.

"How the heck did you get out of those ties?"

"Best you ask Maddie." Ethan gave her an admiring glance.

She shrugged. "It's just another one of the little tricks I learned when I was a kid, and one you don't need to know about." She winked at Ethan, who knew that her late grand-father had shown her how to do stuff like that. Ex-army, gramps had loved to tinker and have the doting audience Maddie proved to be.

Johnny closed his eyes for a minute. "Unbelievable," he uttered, as he got gingerly out of the wreck, holding his chest where the airbag had hit him.

Ethan again motioned with the gun. "Sit down on the grass and don't move a muscle."

"My hay fever is too bad for that," Johnny whined. "Can't I sit in the car?"

Maddie crossed her arms, gritting her teeth against the pain where Johnny had pummeled them. "Really? After all you've done? No, you sit there until the police arrive."

Suzy would have been proud of that chastisement. Not so much Johnny.

"You really are a. . ."

Ethan took a step closer. "I wouldn't finish that sentence if I were you."

"She has no business getting involved. She's not even a deputy," Johnny said sulkily.

He was showing his age now, as he sat, head between his hands. If she hadn't known all the despicable things he'd done, Maddie might have been persuaded to have more sympathy. Big Red, his friends, Maude Oliver, and poor Beth, had been mistreated in so many ways at his hands that she couldn't bring herself to feel more than she did.

The wail of sirens cut through the hissing of the car and Johnny's mutterings, and soon they were surrounded by Ethan's deputies. Ethan was almost as shocked as Johnny.

"How did they know where to find us? The last thing they knew was we'd be at the shed and they were to wait for my signal." he asked.

Maddie shrugged. "I called 911, and I imagine they tracked us. That was the plan, anyway." She went back to the car and found her phone which had fallen under the seat. "You forgot to check my pockets," she said to Johnny.

With a wry grin, Ethan handed over the gun to one of the other deputies. Deputy Jacobs handcuffed Johnny and walked him back up the hill to another car.

Ethan shook his head as he studied her. "You did an amazing job today. As good as any deputy and maybe better than a sheriff. Are you sure you're in the right job?"

Maddie laughed. "Don't talk crazy. Anyone would have done the same thing."

"Yeah, I can imagine Angel leaping over that seat the

way you did, or Suzy having the strength to hold on to a man Johnny's size."

Blushing proudly, she changed the subject. Pointing to the side of his head, she handed him a tissue from her back pocket. "You need some attention to that."

It was his turn to laugh as he took the tissue and dabbed at his face. "Maddie, it's nice to know you're worried about me, but you should see yourself. You're a mess."

She sniffed. "Charming, I'm sure."

"No offence intended. Just take a look at your poor arms for a start."

She shouldn't have. Once she saw the bruises the darn things began to ache with a vengeance.

"Nothing that a good soak and a nap won't fix," she said as they followed the others.

Deputy Jacobs waited by his car with the back door open. Johnny was in the back of another, still angry and feeling sorry for himself. Maddie climbed into Rob Jacob's car and leaned back on the headrest, craving her bed and knowing it was still too early for that. She knew the drill. They'd have to take her to the station to give a statement.

As they drove, Maddie felt proud that they'd cracked the case until she thought of Big Red. Another minute of not knowing if he was okay suddenly seemed unbearable.

"Deputy, all those animals he kidnapped are locked in cages too small for them with no food or water. Please can we go back to the shed he was keeping them in before we drive to the station? It's not that far and besides it's on the way back to Maple Falls."

The deputy turned out to be a dog lover. Appalled by what had happened to the animals he was only too happy to help. Especially when Ethan, who was sitting in the front seat, nodded resignedly at Rob's unspoken question.

"It makes sense. Plus, I'd like to see how our alleged killer got to the shed. There must be a vehicle stowed somewhere and there's bound to be even more evidence inside it." He faced Maddie and winked.

Regardless of the reasons he'd given his deputy, Ethan understood about Big Red, which meant a great deal to her. The deputy turned the car around then radioed the station to tell them about the detour and to request additional transportation for the animals.

When they got back to where they'd left him, Big Red was waiting on the path as if he'd been there all along and was expecting this precise outcome. She called out to him as soon as she could safely open the door, but he wouldn't come. Instead he turned with his tail in the air and strutted back to the shed, looking back a couple of times to ensure they would follow.

Deputy Jacobs stood in wonder when he got to the broken door. "Wow! There are so many in here I recognize. I could just about name all the owners. Funny that we didn't get as many reports."

Maddie picked up Big Red and pushed her face into his neck. "They were promised the pets would be returned for a price and also for their silence."

Rob shook his head. "People never learn that taking the law into their own hands doesn't work, do they?"

Ethan snorted and Rob, understanding precisely what he was alluding to, grinned at Maddie.

"Present company excepted," he said. "Shall we let them out?"

Maddie ignored their teasing, since they were kind of right, and chewed her lip for a moment, before shaking her head.

"Maybe it's not such a good idea to set them free out

here. The door is useless now. Some of them might take off and not know which way home is. Losing them at this stage would be awful. Let's load up the car with any that look like they need immediate attention, then get a truck out here to get the rest. We could give them some fresh water to tide them over."

Jacobs turned to Ethan who nodded, then looked back to Maddie.

"Yes, Boss," he said, cheekily, as he picked up a cage in each hand of lethargic shitzu puppies and took them to the car.

Maddie sniffed, then turned to Ethan. "Perhaps you could bring Sissy? She's older than the rest and Mr. Clayton will be so relieved."

"I certainly can, Boss." He undid the cage and pulled gently on the nervous dog's lead.

Maddie let that ride too, as she filled bowls with water. After such a wonderful outcome, she couldn't wait to see Jed Clayton's face, and those of the others who would get back their loved ones.

Chapter Twenty-Nine

Maddie carried a small cage containing a dog of dubious parentage, flea-bitten, and sad looking. She turned back at the car feeling guilty about not taking more. Ethan saw her concern.

"The others will be collected as soon as possible. In fact, I'll send word to the vets right now. They have a big van that could take most of them in one trip."

"That's a great idea. The sooner we get them away from here the better," she smiled, as Big Red sauntered up the path.

She chose to imagine he had left the animals with the knowledge they would all be rescued soon. He stopped outside the car to check his new friends which were coming with them, were okay. Then he jumped inside, waiting for Maddie to join him on the back seat. When she settled the cage securely on the floor, he curled up onto her lap, his head nuzzling her chin. She wished she had food for him, but her purse with treats was back in Ethan's car which was inconveniently wrapped around a tree.

She gave a shudder when she thought of another

outcome that might have meant these animals were never found. Big Red licked her cheek with his rasping tongue. She agreed with him, there was no point in dwelling on that.

Ethan closed the doors, leaving the windows open a crack. "I won't be long. I'm just going to search the area better than we did last time. Jacobs, stay with Ms. Flynn."

She watched him search the shrubs surrounding the shed through half-closed eyes. At one stage he disappeared into a dark space to the left of the shed. It was overgrown with vines and weeds and must have gone back a way. When he came out he had a huge grin, which stayed with him on the walk back to the car.

"You're looking very pleased with yourself," she said, as he got in and put on his seatbelt.

"Hopefully you'll be just as pleased. Honey is tucked up in that tangle of vines back there."

She gasped. "Really? That's wonderful. Wait. Is she okay?"

His smile faded. "I'd say she needs a bit of attention. She has a dent on her hood."

Maddie gulped. "I guess we know what caused that?"

"Don't think about that right now."

She nodded, although it was difficult. "Are you leaving her here?"

"I'm afraid she'll be here for several days. She's a big piece of evidence. Detective Jones will come and check her out and there will be police swarming all over the place. She'll be safe enough."

Maddie digested that as they headed back. Exhausted, and seemingly happy about their rescue, the animals slept, while Maddie's face stayed buried in Big Red's fur. Judging by the purring, he didn't mind at all.

When they eventually walked into the station, they were immediately surrounded by the deputies and the Detective.

"Maddie cracked the case again," Jacobs told them.

Rob Jacobs was Ethan's top deputy. He'd taken some time to warm to her, but since she'd help solve the case of the mayor's murder a few months back, he had changed his tune. Now, whenever he saw her, he was always pleasant and chatty. Still, she hadn't expected this level of gushing from the otherwise stoic man, which was attracting even more attention. A small crowd filled the entryway.

"It was a team effort," she insisted, pushing her face into Big Red's fur again, at the impromptu round of applause.

Ethan was beside her holding Sissy's lead. He put a hand on her arm to steer her down to his office, but stopped after a step to call out to everyone in the room in general.

"If you're not busy, please head out to Rob's car and bring in the animals. Be careful, some of them don't seem to appreciate we just saved their lives and are a little annoyed at still being captive."

"Understandable," Rob said as he went to pat Big Red, who was still as fussy as ever when it came to who was given that privilege, and growled loudly.

The deputy jumped back. "I get the message, big fella. I'll leave this one with you and go get more."

When they got to Ethan's office Detective Jones was there. He stood. "Well done, Sheriff and you too, Ms. Flynn. We'll talk soon, but I'd like to take a look at the crime scene right now. I'll head back with one of the deputies, if you think you can handle things here?"

"I think Johnny Chisholm can cool his heels for a bit while we take care of the animals, then I'll interview him, unless you want me to wait?"

"You go ahead. From what I've seen you have things in hand."

Maddie smiled, but was barely listening. There was still so much to do. She put the cage with the scruffy looking dog on the floor. She wondered why the poor thing had been taken, because he certainly didn't look like a pedigree.

It was nice to be somewhere a little quieter. Maddie took a seat in front of the desk and Sissy slumped onto the carpet beside her, while Big Red settled onto her lap. She rubbed his fur, which was matted, and he arched his back for more.

Ethan sat on the corner of his desk and they stared at each other for a moment.

"Well," he said with a grin, "So much for not interfering."

She laughed, unapologetically. "It will be a big job reuniting these guys with their owners. Do you want me to start calling? Most of them have tags on with numbers, and if the vet is coming here it would be good for them all to have a check-up as soon as possible," she suggested.

Ethan grinned. "I noticed the tags, and it would be a big help. If you don't feel you've done enough?"

"It would be a pleasure. Almost a reward when you think about it." She smiled. "There are going to be some very happy people."

He grinned back. "Thanks to you, that's true. I'll find a spare desk with a phone and a pad to write down the details."

Just then Deputy Funnel entered, looking decidedly embarrassed. Maddie was too happy to hold a grudge and she offered a smile. The woman smiled back with relief.

"Sir, the vet has picked up the animals, but says he hasn't enough room at his clinic. He wants to bring the animals to the station and is happy to check them out here for free. His van will have all the supplies he needs to do that and he assured me it will save time."

Ethan heaved a massive sigh.

He looked so tired and his head must have been pounding after that knock to it. Maddie worried that he might have a concussion as well as all the bruises from the abuse and the crash.

"Okay," he said. "Let's do that. Set up some cells for them with water and send someone to get food for cats and dogs. Oh, and seed for the birds." He gave Maddie a wry smile. "It looks like it might be a very long night."

"I can call the Girlz to help out?"

He nodded appreciatively. "Perfect. More hands will get this done a lot sooner, and I'll be tied up with the kidnapper. I'm sure you can handle it, and you may as well use my desk until they arrive. If you need anything, just give Deputy Funnel a yell. She seems to be your new best friend."

The wink he gave her made her laugh, especially when the deputy turned a shade of pink Angel would have admired. When the two of them left, she called her friend while beginning the list with the animals she knew—with a large grin on her face.

Angel picked up on the first ring and relayed the message to Gran, Laura, and Suzy who were all waiting at the cottage with Beth. They were pleased to hear she was safe and delighted the animals were saved. She could hear them chattering, wanting to know details, so Angel put her on speakerphone. Once Maddie told them what was needed, without hesitation, they promised to be there soon.

They arrived at the same time as the vets' truck and together they helped get all the animals housed in the cells.

The smaller ones and the birds remained in cages to prevent their escape. It wasn't perfect, but would have to do. Hopefully, it was a short time before the animals were checked and collected.

Maddie was given a small desk downstairs and Big Red came too. There was no way she wanted him out of her sight and he seemed to feel the same way.

With her lists drawn up and the girls help she began making notes on each animal, taking details from their tags. She had just finished all of that when Jed Clayton arrived. He was excited, his eyes darting around the cells, until they landed on her.

"Maddie, thank you so much. I don't see her. Where's Sissy?" his voice rose in panic.

Maddie jumped up and smiled gently. "Sissy is safe upstairs, asleep under the sheriff's desk. She's plum tuckered out and as we already knew who she belonged to, I let her be. Come on, let's go get her."

She left her post to Suzy and took him to the offices upstairs with Big Red on her heels. As soon as he walked through the door Sissy bounded up to him. Tears ran unchecked down the old man's cheeks and Maddie could feel her eyes welling up. She had too much to do to succumb to them just yet, so she left the man and his dog to their touching reunion and went to call the next number on her list.

Suzy had split the lists evenly, and before an hour was up they had contacted all the owners they had tags for. With one exception. Make that three. One was Maude Oliver's little dog and the other two had no ID and were the only ones without microchips.

Maddie tapped her pen on the desk, as she studied the Shitzu puppies. The vet had checked them already so they were free to go. But to where? "Are you sure they don't have any tags?"

"None. I'd guess they're barely eight weeks old," Angel said.

"What's wrong?" Rob Jacobs asked as he came along the hall.

Maddie pointed to the two puppies that Laura and Angel held. The little rascals were alternating between licks and nips at whatever they could reach, making the women giggle.

"We don't know who they belong to. I don't remember any reports on them being missing, do you?"

He shook his head. "I'm pretty sure not. There were far fewer reports than there were pets."

"I guess the owners had their reasons, but what on earth will we do with them?" Laura's voice cracked.

"I'm too busy with the school and committees to look after puppies," Suzy said firmly.

"And I'm working six days in the salon," grimaced Angel. "I sure hope that isn't going to get worse."

She gave Maddie a telling look, obviously referring to Beth, who'd turned out to be a great asset to the salon but might now be doing time somewhere else, depending on how deep she was involved in all of this.

Deputy Jacobs wandered across the room and studied the adorable pair. They gave him wide-eyed innocent looks and yawned simultaneously. Their full bellies making them look like furry round balls.

He grinned. "My job's busy too, but I was thinking about getting a dog. Only I didn't want it to be lonely. I guess two of them would keep each other company, and they certainly look related. It would be a shame to split them up."

"Their owners might turn up," Maddie warned, knowing that once you loved an animal it was hard to say goodbye.

He frowned, then shrugged. "They might, but just in case they don't, these two deserve a bit of TLC, don't they?"

"That is so kind of you, Deputy," Laura gushed.

"It's n-n-nothing," he stammered, suddenly not the self-possessed deputy he usually was.

After swapping looks, Angel and Maddie turned away from the charming little interchange, secretly pleased.

Finally, once all the animals were checked and picked up, and Maddie had given her statement to the Detective, Ethan drove her and Big Red home. Happy, but tired, the Girlz had already left with Gran and they'd all been given the thanks of the department.

Once inside, Maddie loaded up Big Red's bowls, opening a gourmet tin of fish and giving him milk as a treat.

"You don't think he had enough at the station?" Ethan asked as he put the kettle on.

"Probably, but he deserves a bit of spoiling, after risking his life to stay with his friends."

"Reminds me of someone else I know."

She knew he was half-teasing, but she wanted to relish the good that had come from today. "I know I'm a pain in the backside, but can you let it go for now?"

"Sure," was all he said, as he made tea for her and coffee for himself.

They sat in companionable silence while Big Red sampled his treats, then yawned and went to sit by the bottom of the stairs.

"Do you think he's trying to tell us something?" Ethan grinned.

"Undoubtedly. He's the boss, after all."

"Then I should go. But first, I have to say thank you again for what you did today and tonight. I can't believe that not only did you set us free, but you captured Johnny."

His hand stretched across the table and she put hers in his.

"That's a bit of an exaggeration since you were right by my side. Quite frankly, I didn't want to die," she said openly, while her heart beat faster with their hands entwined as they were.

"Neither did I, but your reflexes when you dove between the seats boggles my mind." His thumb caressed hers.

Big Red jumped onto her lap and, reaching over the table, he nudged Ethan's hand away. They both laughed, and Ethan sat back.

"You know, I think a great deal about you, Maddie?"

Her voice cracked. "We've been friends a long time."

"That's true." He gave her an appraising look. "I don't think life with you could ever be boring, and I feel we have more here than friendship. I've been patient, and Big Red is home, so could we try dating now?"

She raised an eyebrow. "Try?"

He gave her a wry smile. "I might not be able to keep up with your antics."

That made her laugh. "The petnapper has been caught. Hopefully Mrs. Fitzgibbon's blackmailer will be too. There couldn't possibly be any more drama after all that?"

"Hmmm. I can't think of anything right at this moment, but I wish you hadn't asked that without touching wood, or something equally suitable. And, I reserve the right to comment sometime in the future, should that change. I feel like I know you better than all those years ago, but one thing is certain, peace and quiet has never been your way."

Maddie wasn't sure whether she should be offended, but that twinkle in his eye, and the fact that what he said had a modicum of truth ringing through it, made her smile.

"I accept your conditions."

He grinned. "Now that we have that sorted, there wouldn't be anything to eat, would there? I didn't get time to eat any of Gran's food, and I'm famished. Detective work sure creates a hunger."

"Yes, it does." She stood and bent to give him a quick kiss on the lips as she headed to the walk in, loving the surprised look in his eyes, and hoping the following one of eagerness was for another kiss and not one of her lemon cupcakes.

This day was important because Big Red and the other animals were safe, but also for the fact that Ethan and she were making progress in this up and down relationship.

Yes, she nodded to herself, their own cold case was getting decidedly warmer.

Chapter Thirty

Scones. Two flavors and four women, including Maddie. It was going to be a long, fun evening. She knew this for sure because her world was how it should be. With Big Red watching over the proceedings once more and getting more than his fair share of attention, she knew she was beaming.

They had been inseparable since his return, and every minute of today she had been aware of where he was. Not that he went too far, and even his visits to the garden were out of necessity.

She was ready to celebrate, and the cooking class, a day later than usual, couldn't be better for doing just that. Everyone had their favorite drink and was raring to go. The Girlz had picked their own spaces weeks ago and stuck to them. That sort of orderliness suited Maddie perfectly.

"Okay bakers, three cups of sifted flour and six teaspoons of baking powder. Add your butter, and using your fingertips rub it in so the mixture looks like bread-crumbs. Excellent. Let's add the sugar to the sweet ones, and the salt to the savory. Done?"

They nodded.

"Now we add the raisins or cheese. Mix with your hands and make a well in the middle."

"What's a well?" Angel asked.

"A dip in the middle, push the ingredients up the sides a little. Perfect. Add the milk in and mix gently."

Angel screwed her nose up. "This feels gross."

Maddie sighed at her friend's penchant for plastic gloves for baking, knowing that feeling the mixture of anything could make a difference to its perfection, but accepting that she would have to gradually wean Angel off them.

"I think it feels wonderful. Like an artist making a sculpture," Laura insisted.

Maddie held up her own mixture which was a cohesive, not too sticky, lump. "This is what we're after."

They came close to inspect.

"Mine doesn't look like that." Angel pouted.

"Nor mine." Suzy grinned, unfazed.

"Suzy, you need a little more milk. Angel you need a little flour."

When they were done, she showed them how to make balls of the mixture and place them on the trays covered in baking parchment.

"We're nearly there. Push the scones until they are flatter, like mine. For the cheese ones, sprinkle the last of your cheese on top and press down slightly. Sweet scones can be brushed with milk then sprinkle a little sugar on the top."

"I haven't got enough cheese." Angel called out.

Maddy held back another sigh and took her some she had grated earlier for just such an event, knowing full well Angel had been sampling her own stock.

"Remember it's very important to have the oven at the

right temperature before you started baking. I already made sure, so let's put them all in together."

Excitedly they did this and stood back with Big Red at their side, waiting for their next instructions.

"We'll try 10 minutes, then check them. If they need more we leave them, but we don't want them to be stones when they come out, so—keep watching ladies."

She put a timer on, just in case they got chatting, then they loaded the dishwasher and cleaned up.

Angel threw her gloves in the bin, took off the apron that might have more flour than her scones, and was instantly back to her perfect self. "That was pretty easy."

Suzy shook her head in amusement. "If they turn out okay."

"They'll be fine. Another drink anyone?" Maddie asked, already headed to the walk-in.

That brought about a cheer. Then they sat around the table waiting for their baking to be ready. The smell was causing Maddie's stomach to rumble, and she realized she hadn't eaten much today. With everything that happened, she had been making sure that Big Red was eating plenty and had lots of attention. She turned to find him stretched out on a chair by the alcove, fast asleep.

Suzy followed her gaze. "He looks particularly comfortable."

"He sure does."

"How's he been?" Angel asked.

"Amazing. He kept very close all night and this morning, but once he was outside he seemed to appreciate that he was home for good. He even chased a butterfly and got off the ground," Maddie recalled the moment with delight.

Laura watched him fondly. "Maybe all that action and weight loss has given him another lease on life."

"I think you might be right. I can't help spoiling him right now, but I will cut down on his treats starting tomorrow. Hopefully Gran and Laura will get the memo."

"Me?" Laura said, with fake innocence.

They laughed, knowing that she and Gran were the worst perpetrators.

"So, after we contacted all the owners, and Deputy Jacobs took the puppies, there was only Maude Oliver's dog left, wasn't there?" Suzy asked.

"That's right. I think they were organizing a stay at the animal shelter for her until Maude's family could be contacted. There didn't seem to be any answers from the numbers we have, so it's hard to know if anyone will claim the dog."

"Let's hope they do."

Maddie nodded. "I wondered if I should bring it home, but Big Red needs his one-on-one right now and he's not that fond of dogs anyway."

The timer sounded and the chairs scraped back as they raced to the oven, barely holding back for Maddie to do the honors. Somehow, it seemed to have become a ritual.

"Oh, my," she said as she opened the door.

"Are they burnt?" Angel yelled in her ear in a panic.

"They're perfect." She pulled out the first tray to show them the golden, brown scones.

Angel was practically jumping up and down. "Those are mine. Wow. I can't believe I made them."

One by one, Maddie placed them on the trivets across the bench, amidst oohs and ahhs. The faces of her friends glowed with this small accomplishment and Maddie grinned. She had to admit, their attempts were getting pretty good.

Angel picked one up, juggling in her hands, since they

were still too hot. She looked at Maddie imploringly. "I guess we should taste them."

"Of course." She pulled out some plates, knives, and butter. "Perhaps you could cut up another one each so we can try each other's?"

They agreed, and with no finesse they tucked into their respective scones while Maddie made tea, because one couldn't eat a scone without tea. Everyone knew that.

She took the pot to the table and collected a tea set for each of them. One by one they filtered back to their seats.

"Well?" Maddie asked, as she poured.

"I'm amazed. They're like store bought ones. Dad will be so surprised," Suzy gushed.

"Which one was the best?" Angel asked when Maddie had sampled each one.

"They are all good," she said sincerely. "I got you to try each other's so you could get an idea of how another batch can vary slightly."

"Why is that?" Angel asked.

"It depends on several things. The ingredients. The mixture—if it's too wet or too dry—how much you handle it, and how rough you are. And, naturally, the cooking time."

"Mine just melted in my mouth." Laura gave a cheeky grin to her fellow students.

Angel and Suzy poked their tongues out, while Maddie laughed.

"Are you confident you could make this at home?"

They nodded, with Laura the more certain.

"Excellent. Did you bring your books so that you can stick in this recipe and make any amendments or notes?"

Dutifully they brought out their notebooks. Laura and Suzy's were plain workbooks like a child uses in school, but

Angel's was a work of art, with lots of bling decorating the fuchsia cover.

Angel knew they were laughing at it, but she didn't care. "They aren't too expensive to make, which is nice," she said as she added a couple of pink hearts for good measure from a sheet of stickers she kept at the back of it.

Maddie decided to give them a little history to round out the lesson. "Scones were a staple in years gone by in England, and still today you can add or omit ingredients depending on what is available at the time. Plain ones can be dipped in soup and sweet ones can be a desert or a snack. I often add a yellow bell-pepper or onion to my cheese ones and sometimes ham if I want a more substantial meal but don't want to cook meat."

As they wrote furiously, there was a knock at the door and Ethan walked in. He was in uniform minus his hat, which he held. It looked in remarkable condition considering his penchant for twisting the poor thing. Ethan was also in good shape, apart from his face which matched hers in the bruising department, with the added bonus of an egg-shaped lump on his forehead.

"Good evening ladies. I don't want to interrupt, but I heard you'd be together tonight and I thought it would be easier to say what I need to."

"Are we in trouble?" asked Suzy.

"Not at all." He looked at them warily, then clearly deciding that it was simply a question and not an indication they were actually doing something wrong, smiled in relief. "I've come to thank you all personally for the help in returning the pets. I know it was a lot of work and it certainly freed up my deputies to tackle everything else pertaining to the case. You did it very efficiently and probably a darn sight faster than we could have."

The Girlz glowed under the praise.

"It was a pleasure, Sheriff. Making the calls and then handing over a beloved animal must be one of the most rewarding things I've ever done," Angel gushed.

The other's agreed loudly, and Maddie had to concur. It had been pretty cool, if emotional.

"You might like to know how things are going. Unofficially, of course."

"Of course," they chimed.

Ethan grinned. "Luke's brother was up to his neck with Mickey Findlay. He not only confessed, but explained how his father insisted he get some business experience by working for Mickey. I'm pretty sure, when he suggested it, his father didn't have what they did in mind."

The women nodded, waiting for more.

"What started out as scare tactics around the election, ending up with Johnny getting greedy. He thought the owners would keep paying indefinitely, but some called his bluff and to his credit, he couldn't kill those pets."

"Hmmm. He showed no such compunction with us?" Maddie interjected.

"It would seem so, but he was running scared and Mickey had washed his hands of him. He had no idea how to get himself out of it. With them both trying to blame the other, and the blackmailing charge from Irene Fitzgibbons, it will take a pretty good lawyer to get this to go away."

As much as she liked to turn the other cheek, Maddie couldn't be happier that Mickey was finally getting caught. "But what about the original murder?" she asked.

"The death outside of Destiny? He was the owner of a missing pet, but it was an accident. He drove too fast for the conditions and lost control."

Maddie was glad that it wasn't murder. Now, she had

one more important question she'd put off asking. "What about Luke?"

Ethan smiled. "Turns out he's a bit of a hero. He knew nothing about his brother's involvement, but found out that Johnny was hurting Beth. Initially, he gave her your leftover bagels thinking they were for her. When she broke down and told him they were for the pets he didn't know what to do, but it was Luke who told her to come and tell you everything."

Maddie's heart lifted again. She was certain all along he was innocent, but sometimes facts got in the way of the truth. "What about Beth?"

"I'm not sure. There are extenuating circumstances, of course. With her own life in jeopardy, I daresay she did the best she could, but she should have told someone."

Angel sucked in a breath. "I'll be a witness to the bruising and the arguments, if I can?"

"You'll all likely be called to give evidence."

Suzy tutted. "I do feel for those two. Are they back home?"

"Yes. Their parents came for them."

She raised an eyebrow. "I bet that wasn't a picnic for any of them."

"No, but Detective Jones handled it well. He spoke to them all about the gravity of the situation, and both mothers broke down. I think Beth's days of living rough are done, and Luke's father will be having a good look at his parenting skills."

"Maybe he could find a way to be proud of Luke."

"Let's hope so. By the way, we found Johnny's bike among the trees where he'd tossed it over the hedge. With a bag of bagels in a backpack. Beth's, I believe."

Maddie smiled. "So those are the missing pieces. He

swapped his broken-down bike for Honey, then accidentally killed Maude—or so he says. Thanks so much for coming to tell us. I know I'll sleep better tonight."

Ethan smiled, his dimple flashing non-stop, and Maddie could feel her cheeks warming.

"Would you like to sample our baking? It would be nice to get an outsider's opinion and a Sheriff never lies." Angel pulled a seat up to the counter for him.

He looked at Maddie for approval. "I don't want to interrupt."

"It's okay, we've finished. Sit down and I'll make more tea while the Girlz butter you some scones. Or would you like coffee?"

He grinned. "Now, that's an offer this Sheriff can't refuse."

Maddie made his coffee and more tea for the rest, then sat back and let her friends fuss over him, and when he had sampled them all and declared them excellent, they finally let him be. He stood and patted his stomach with a groan.

"I had better get home before I burst out of these clothes, and Amy might be fussing if I'm gone too long."

Maddie was walking him to the door when he delivered this, and she stilled. "Amy?"

He turned with a blush to his cheeks. "Maude Oliver's Amy. We tried to find her a home. I thought Maude's sister might take her, but she breeds Siamese cats, and they don't like dogs apparently. What could I do?"

Her mouth twitched at his perplexed look, as if he was still surprised by the outcome. "So, you're looking after Amy?"

Ethan grimaced as he looked back at their audience, who were silently awaiting the answer. "Ahhh. Not exactly. I'm going to keep her."

"Really?"

"What's wrong with that? I have a house plant that's still alive."

She was trying so hard not to laugh at his defensiveness. "I think it's wonderful. Amy seems a lovely little thing. You'll be good company for each other."

He took her arm as gently as he could, mindful of the bruises that were already colorful yellows and purples, and pulled her outside. He also dropped his voice. "I think it's high time I stopped being such a loner. Maybe now that things are calming down you might like to have dinner with me?"

Maddie was never more aware of the changes in Ethan, and in herself, and she couldn't help thinking they were all for the better.

"Give me a couple of days to unwind, then ask me again."

"Really?"

Ethan's eyes twinkled and she nodded. He dropped a quick kiss on her lips, with a cheeky grin, he went down the path with a noticeable spring in his step. She had the urge to call him back for a repeat performance, maybe with a little more substance, until she remembered the Girlz. As she came through the door, there was a mad scramble to regain their seats as they tried to look innocent.

"Were you lot looking out the window?"

Angel was in the process of shaking her head, but her mouth opened as well. "Absolutely. And I think it's fabulous that you two are dating again."

"Hold the phone! We're only having dinner."

"I guess a girl has to eat," said Suzy with a wink.

"Go home the lot of you!"

With lots of nudging and giggles, they left. Laura turned at the gate.

"I told you the bagels were a good idea."

Maddie shook her head as she went inside. Who would have thought how important the innocent bagel could be? It may have even helped keep the animals alive, thanks to Beth and Luke. She hoped they would be back at work very soon, because despite all the things they'd done wrong, their intentions had been good. And, like Gran said, everyone deserved a second chance.

Big Red jumped from the chair and stretched. Then he strutted to the bottom of the stairs, turned, and gave her a long look.

The boss had spoken, and there was no mystery around it being time for bed.

Thanks so much for reading Bagels and Blackmail. I hope you enjoyed it!

If you did...
1 Help other people find this book by leaving a review.

2 Sign up for my new release e-mail, so you can find out about the next book as soon as it's available.

3 Come like my Facebook page.

4 Visit my website for the very best deals.

5 Keep reading for an excerpt from Cookies and Chaos.

Cookies and Chaos

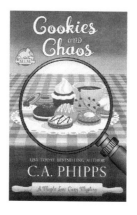

Maddie frowned. "Bernie won't be too happy that someone's messed up the green this way."

The sheriff towered over her 5'6" form. To see his face, she had to block what he didn't of the fall sun with her hand.

"He was the one who told me about it, and no he's not amused. Looks like a van took a joy ride."

She bent over the marks to see what he saw. "How can you tell it what type of vehicle it was?"

He pointed at the marks. "The width of the tires, and how deep they've sunk into the grass. It must have had a considerable load in it."

He spoke to her as he would one of his deputies and a trickle of pleasure ran through her. Was that weird?

"They've driven over the path there and come back the same way but on a slightly different trajectory." He pointed.

"Then they've headed across the park. Why would they want to do that?" she asked.

He shrugged. "That's the second question."

She tapped her thigh. "The first is where were they going?"

He gave her an appraising look. "Exactly. If we can figure out the where, we'll eventually get to the why."

She stood up, unable to hide her excited and hopeful tone. "We?"

"I meant the department 'we'." He gave her a wry grin.

She screwed up her nose. "Sure, you did."

"Maddie." Ethan warned, in his growly voice, which resembled more of a teddy bear than anything scary.

"What? It's not a murder, is it?" she asked, innocently.

"Definitely not," he said, without conviction.

Having known the Sheriff since they were children, she knew when he was worried. "Did something else happen?"

"I don't know what you mean."

She ignored his terrible attempt at outrage. "What was it? More tire tracks? Another vehicle? Maybe a crash?"

"Calm down." He sighed, looking around them, then pulled her close. "Since there won't be any peace any other way, I'll tell you what I know."

248

Need to know what happens next? Get your copy of Book 3 in the Maple Lane Cozy Mystery Series, Cookies and Chaos now!

Recipes

These recipes are ones I use all the time and have come down the generations from my mum, grandmother, and some I have adapted from other recipes. Also, I now have my husband's grandmother's recipe book. Exciting! I'll be bringing some of them to life very soon.

Just a wee reminder, that I am a New Zealander. Occasionally I may have missed converting into ounces and pounds for my American readers.

My apologies for that, and please let me know—if you do try them—how they turn out.

Cheryl x

Bagels

Ready in: 2hrs
Makes: 12 Bagels

Ingredients

1 1/2 cups water
2 packages yeast
1 1/2 ounces sugar
1/2 ounce salt
3 1/2 cups bread flour
2 quarts water, to boil
1 egg white
cinnamon (optional)
raisins (optional)
poppy seed (optional)
dried onion or garlic (optional)
sesame seeds (Optional)

Instructions

1 Mix yeast, sugar and warm water together and let stand 3
minutes.

2 Mix 2 cups of flour with the salt in a large bowl and add the yeast mixture.

3 Stir until combined and slowly mix in the rest of the flour (If making cinnamon raisin bagels, add these to dough now).

4 Knead on a floured surface for 5 minutes, adding additional flour if needed, dough should be firm. Place dough in a greased bowl, cover and let rise until double.

5 After rising punch down and divide dough into 12 balls. Allow to rest for 4 minutes.

6 Bring 2 quarts of water to boil.

7 With your thumb, make a hole in each ball of dough and pull open about 2 inches, making a bagel shape.

8 Preheat oven to 180°C or 350°F.

9 Place the shaped dough onto a cookie sheet and cover for 10 minutes.

10 Lower heat under water for it to be simmering. Drop 2 or 3 bagels at a time into the water for about 45 seconds, turning each once. Drain and place on greased baking sheets.

11 Brush tops with beaten egg white and top with optional toppings.

12 Bake for 35 minutes, turning once for even browning. Bagels are done when they are golden brown and shiny.

Scones

Ingredients
Plain

3 cups of plain flour
6 teaspoons of baking powder
1/2 teaspoon of salt
1 3/4 ounces of butter
1 cup of milk
Preheat oven to 180°C or 350°F

Instructions

1 Sift flour baking powder and salt into a bowl. Using a knife, cut in butter until the flour mixture looks like breadcrumbs.

2 Make a well in the middle of the mixture and pour in milk. Lightly mix with hands until it forms a ball.

3 Split ball into 12 even smaller balls and place on baking tray. Flatten slightly and brush with milk.

4 Bake for 10-12 minutes

Plain scones have been served as a Devonshire tea in

England for decades. It is usual to serve them with your favorite jam and a good dollop of whipped cream.

Cheese

As above but add 1/2 cups of grated cheese to flour mixture prior to adding milk.

When you have flattened them, instead of brushing with milk top with a little more grated cheese.

Gran likes to add some chopped capsicum and onion to her cheese scones, but you could also add ham or spring onions.

Sweet

Use the same recipe for the plain scones but add 1/2 cup of sugar to flour mixture and 1/2 cup of sultanas or raisins before you add the milk.

Also by C. A. Phipps

Midlife Potions - Paranormal Cozy Mysteries

Witchy Awakening

Witchy Hot Spells

Witchy Flash Back

Witchy Bad Blood - preorder now!

The Cozy Café Mysteries

Sweet Saboteur

Candy Corruption

Mocha Mayhem

Berry Betrayal

Deadly Double-Dip

The Maple Lane Cozy Mysteries

Sugar and Sliced - Maple Lane Prequel

Apple Pie and Arsenic

Bagels and Blackmail

Cookies and Chaos

Doughnuts and Disaster

Eclairs and Extortion

Fudge and Frenemies

Gingerbread and Gunshots

Honey Cake and Homicide - preorder now!

Beagle Diner Cozy Mysteries

Beagles Love Cupcake Crimes

Beagles Love Steak Secrets

Beagles Love Muffin But Murder

Beagles Love Layer Cake Lies - preorder now!

Please note: Most are also available in paperback and some in audio.

Remember to join Cheryl's Cozy Mystery newsletter.

There's a free recipe book waiting for you. ;-)

Cheryl also writes romance as Cheryl Phipps.

About the Author

'Life is a mystery. Let's follow the clues together.'

C. A. Phipps is a USA Today best-selling author from beautiful New Zealand. Cheryl lives in a quiet suburb with her wonderful husband, whom she married the moment she left school (yes, they were high school sweethearts). With three married children and seven grandchildren to keep her busy when she's not writing, there is just enough space for a crazy mixed breed dog who stole her heart! She enjoys family times, baking, rambling walks, and her quest for the perfect latte.

Check out her website http://caphipps.com

facebook.com/authorcaphipps

x.com/CherylAPhipps

instagram.com/caphippsauthor

Made in the USA
Middletown, DE
18 August 2024